TOM PENNY

A TOM PENNY ADVENTURE

TOM PENNY

TONY GERMAN

Cover by
Regolo Ricci

Scholastic Canada Ltd.

Scholastic Canada Ltd.
123 Newkirk Road, Richmond Hill, Ontario, Canada L4C 3G5

Scholastic Inc.
730 Broadway, New York, NY 10003, USA

Ashton Scholastic Pty Limited
PO Box 579, Gosford, NSW 2250, Australia

Ashton Scholastic Limited
Private Bag 1, Penrose, Auckland, New Zealand

Scholastic Publications Ltd.
Villiers House, Clarendon Avenue,
Leamington Spa, Warwickshire CV32 5PR, UK

Canadian Cataloguing in Publication Data

German, Tony 1942-
    Tom Penny

ISBN 0-590-73610-8

I. Title.

PS8563.E69T65   1990   jC813'.54   C90-094904-X
PZ7.G475To 1990

7 6 5 4 3 2   Printed in Canada   1 2 3 4 5/9
                        Manufactured by Webcom Limited

*To Sage
for all her work, her patience
and her support.*

The Tom Penny Adventures

Tom Penny
River Race
The Grand Canal

Contents

1. Edgeham

We lived in Edgeham which is not far off the London Road after it has finished its long climb up Portsdown Hill. The Hill is a long open grassy ridge really, rolling high up behind Portsmouth Harbour. You could sometimes snare rabbits there and I'd gone out after church that Sunday to try my luck.

Warm and lazy I lay stretched out in the spring sunshine, waiting for a rabbit to catch itself. The grass had that fresh green smell and the bird calls said summer was on the way.

It was my favourite spot. I could keep half an eye on the burrows along the bank and at the same time look down across the whole great stretch of Portsmouth Harbour.

Hulks of wooden warships lay swinging to the tide. Beyond them sprawled the city, spewing smoke. A forest of masts and yards was packed in by the harbour mouth and beyond that lay the sea.

And what lay beyond the sea? I'd listened from my bed to the rumbling voices of my father and an occasional friend or two talking over old times around our kitchen fire. They had all been soldiers — or sailors — in the wars against Bonaparte. Their tales of other lands made stuff for daydreams, and the drowsy day crept by.

I can remember a sudden chill waking me from my doze. A gusty wind swept the grass in waves and the sun ducked behind a low black cloud. A wall of rain moved in across the harbour and I shook myself and turned towards Edgeham.

The storm caught me as I passed the Manor and the old Admiral's home-farm building and I was soaking wet by the time I passed the inn. I sloshed across the green, scattering the ducks, passed the old stone church and ducked through my hole in the hedge. A hundred yards along the lane I vaulted the wall and dashed straight to our kitchen door.

I burst in, puffing hard and wet through, and hung my empty game-bag on the peg. There was Mother fussing with the kettle, Father poking up the fire and a lean, white-haired man settled down in the chair by the hearth. We had a visitor.

"Ah! Tom," said Father. He turned. "My younger boy, Tom, sir." It was the Admiral, Sir Henry Hardcastle. Our landlord.

"Yes indeed," said the Admiral gruffly. "We've met, young man, we've met. It could just have been you and another young ruffian I nearly caught fishing in my stream last week, eh?" He paused. "That idiot gamekeeper of mine is neither tough enough on you village scallywags nor quick enough, but I keep my eyes open." My heart sank. "By the way, did you catch anything?" His face was stern and I began to stutter and stammer.

"Well sir, you see, I —"

The Admiral's eyes crinkled, and he burst into a laugh. "Come now, Tom — I won't put you in gaol! Just be sure if you do catch a trout you bring it to your mother here. If you catch two, bring one to me!" He looked at Father. "He's a chip off you, Penny, to be sure. Fine young fellow, growing up to be a proper soldier — with all their thieving habits, eh?"

He laughed again with great good humour, then said, "Penny, young Tom should hear what I have to say to you. Send him off for dry clothes — and yes, Mrs. Penny, I'd enjoy that cup of tea. Thank you kindly."

My heart stopped thumping. By the time I was dry, dressed in my Sunday clothes and back in the kitchen, Father and the Admiral were relaxed with their tea and their pipes. Mother sat by the table, smoothing her apron, still rather ill at ease. I sat down beside her.

The Admiral always seemed so ferocious from afar, with his lined face and hawk-nose, but he smiled at me through a cloud of smoke.

"This," he said to Father, "is every bit as much for Tom and your boy Will as it is for you and your wife, Penny — maybe more so. Yes indeed! It's the next generation that counts and the next. It just happens, young Tom," he said to me, "that I was caught in the rain like you. So I knocked on your door and here I am enjoying your father's hearth and your mother's tea and your good company. How old are you, Tom?"

"Fourteen next birthday, sir," I told him.

"Same age I was when I joined my first ship as a midshipman. Old *Valiant* — seventy-four guns. You know, Tom, I was scared stiff. Always the same, starting something new, always the same. There," he said, "I shouldn't be giving you advice, young fellow, just you follow your father here."

He turned to Father. "You know of course, Penny, that the Duke of Wellington has become Prime Minister?"

"Aye sir," said Father, "and high time we had someone in charge in old England."

"Agreed, Penny, agreed," said the Admiral. "If anyone can pull this country together it will be the Duke, and God bless him, I say. But we are in a bad way, a really bad way, and you and Mrs. Penny here know it just as well as I do.

"Look now," he went on. "I'll be all right, and so will people like me who have land and property. Oh yes, I hear all the talk about the taxes ruining the families with the money and how there will be no more investment and no more development in the colonies and how England will sink and I say 'Nonsense!' because there is plenty of spirit here.

4

"All the same, Penny, prices go up and up and work is hard to find. The machines in the new manufactories are putting people out of work more and more every day — and who's to buy all the goods they turn out, eh?"

Father broke in. "Like that threshing machine you bought last autumn, sir. You know, some nigh starved this winter because they didn't get your threshing work?"

"Yes, Penny. I know. And I wish it could be some other way. But this is 1829. Our lives are changing, and that's a fact — steam tugboats in the harbours, and these locomotive-engines on the railways. It's all progress. We'll be better off in the long haul, I daresay, but in the meantime there's upset and suffering, and — begad, Penny! Makes a man almost wish for the old days, eh? Nothing like a war!"

The Admiral's lean old face was alive. He sat forward in his chair, elbows on his knees and he wagged a bony finger.

"Fight Bonaparte." His finger beat out the words, "Fight Bonaparte — that's all. Simple enough. Your father remembers, Tom. He was at Waterloo. An Englishman knew he was an Englishman and he knew what he had to do. Not like today." He shook his head and sat back. "In Parliament it's all 'Reform . . . Reform. Let the Fleet rot, let the farmers starve.'"

Father followed the Admiral's words, frowning to himself.

"A man has to be thankful for what he does have, sir." He paused. "I know you do the best you can for us fellows — not like some of the landlords. It's hard times right enough. But we're better off here than most."

"You're right, Penny, you're right. London is a cesspool. Crime everywhere, prisons and poorhouses full, urchins roaming the streets in bands, filching anything they can get their hands on. Portsmouth is not much better." He looked around at Mother. "We are quite peaceful in Edgeham, Mrs. Penny, but it won't be long, in my opinion, before we'll see the same kind of thing here. Besides," he said, "what is there for young Tom, eh? Working on someone else's land? Maybe he'll get a trade to work to. Yes — I got your Will into his apprenticeship in the dockyard — but now it's a different story. If Tom does get a trade, what then?"

He lit a spill from the fire and sucked his pipe alive. "Now, besides being an old war-horse friend of the Duke's, I'm also the Justice of the Peace hereabouts, and I received yesterday from Whitehall a letter concerning a new land grant in Canada. The Duke wants to see men like you, old soldiers and sailors, given a chance to take up land just as you could have right after the Wars. There were many who did at that time, of course. And thousands went out from Scotland and Ireland, too.

"Oh! There are people there all right, but

there's room for thousands more, millions perhaps. And look here, Penny," he said and he leaned over and tapped Father on the knee. "If we in England don't take up the land out there, why the Americans will, and you can lay your life on that. Men like you who know how to farm and how to fight too, when the time comes. You're the kind we need.

"No point in us sending out the parish poor. Most of them don't know how to work. Mind you, it would be good to see the last of 'em. But they're bone lazy — I suppose we look after them too well, eh?"

Father pursed his lips and said nothing for a moment. The crease deepened between his eyes. "Well sir," he said, "I was in America with the 99th Regiment in the war against the Yankees in '12 and '13. I could have taken up land there and then and not come back to England at all. But back I come — and glad I am, sir — got married then," he smiled at Mother. "It's a hard, wild, lonely land they have there — and cold. Six months of the year there's naught but ice and snow. Summertime, it's stinking hot. Mud in spring — and mosquitoes! Can't for the life o' me understand how they get along there at all."

He poked the fire into a blaze, put another log on and raised an eyebrow at Mother to get the teapot.

"Here," he said, "we know what we've got. It's not much, maybe, but, still, sir," he looked down into the flames, "there's things in what you've said that a man's got to think about. True enough, I'm just a tenant farmer — and the boys —"

"And you were a Sergeant in the 99th so you're entitled to two hundred acres," said the Admiral, "free and clear. Look here, Penny, I can't order you to go — almost wish I could — but I'll say this. If I were twenty years younger and had no land here in England — and no prospects — and a family growing up to no more prospects than yours, why then, I'd just have to go."

He paused. "No," he said, "that's not fair. Talk is easy. You're the one that has to make the decision. Now, what about your brother? The coachman. I understand he soldiered with you. He'd be entitled too. Four hundred acres would make a nice parcel of land for the Penny family put together." He smiled at us all.

Father nodded: "Right enough, sir."

There was a long silence. The fire crackled softly and the kettle whispered on the hob. The rain had stopped and the roof dripped quietly.

"When a man has his own land, he has something, really has something," and he paused again, groping.

Mother's voice came gentle and firm. "He has hope, William. Hope."

He looked at her, at me, then back to the fire, nodding slowly.

"How long do I have to decide?"

The Admiral smiled, winked at me and said: "I know you'll say yes when the time comes. Now here is the situation. I have the maps which were drawn up by the Crown surveyors in Upper and Lower Canada, showing the new concessions in Fitzroy Township and in Onslow. Some of the lots look to me to be really prime. Specially the ones on the river front. Besides," he said, "the timber stands thereabouts are the finest in the world. Why, the masts and spars and half the timbers for the British Fleet have come from there for years."

His old eyes were shining. It was almost as though he were going himself. "I am sending these maps to Mr. Jeremy Leech, my solicitor, in Portsmouth. He has been appointed Crown agent to advertise these land grants and allocate the lots — first come, first served. There's many a pensioner about Portsmouth, and many of 'em on hard times. I'll write to Leech, and you and your brother can have first pick. In fact you can carry the letter and the maps to him on Wednesday. It's a chance for you. Take it, if you will."

The Admiral stood up, bending his head forward under the beams. "Well now, I must be on my way, rain or no." He turned to Mother. "I thank you, Mrs. Penny, for your welcome. Perhaps the next time I take tea with you it may be in your own parlour — in your own home. And I will count it an honour."

He looked at me, buttoning up his cloak, and

said gravely: "I understand, young Tom Penny, that the trout over there are as big as you are — and just about as difficult to catch!"

He chuckled, winked and let himself out the door.

The lamp flickered and danced, the fire flared up from the draught. The door slammed shut and Mother, Father and I stood looking at each other. Father's forehead was still pulled into a frown. Mother's eyes seemed to glow in the lamplight.

Excitement grew inside me. Our own land — our own land! Across the sea. Wild, wonderful, strange and new. A new land, and we could have some of it.

I said: "Father, can we go?"

2. Portsmouth

On Wednesday, Father collected the letter and maps from the Manor. He and I rode most of the way in to Portsmouth in a farm cart along with a load of hay, and we walked the last half-mile through the narrow, crowded streets.

I rarely got to Portsmouth. Being there was exciting, and I was bursting too with thoughts of our great adventure. I rattled on and on, but Father barely answered. He seemed lost in his own thoughts — as silent as usual.

We came to the Hard. A row of tall buildings stood facing the harbour across a busy street. The cobblestones sloped off into the water, and boats and barges moved in and out with traffic for the ships lying at anchor. It smelled of the sea.

One of a dozen polished brass signs at Number 4 announced "Jeremy Leech, Solicitor."

Inside, the hall was gloomy and dark and it took us a few moments to find another sign directing us upstairs. Footsteps clumped down from overhead and a heavy-set soldier with corporal's stripes barged against us on the narrow stairway. He growled in a bad-tempered sort of way, not looking at us, but scowling as though whatever troubled him was our fault. Father shrugged and watched him stump out the door.

We found Mr. Leech's door and knocked. A wizened little man with a bent back and a narrow, mournful face and surprisingly sharp little eyes opened the door, looked closely at the two of us.

"Well?"

"Letters for Mr. Leech," said Father, "from Sir Henry Hardcastle, at Edgeham."

"Ah yes, you may leave them with me, my good man. Mr. Leech is away until tomorrow afternoon." He held out a long-clawed hand for the letters. Father made no move to give them to him.

There was a pause, then the little man said, "I am Cornelius Twiss, Mr. Leech's confidential clerk."

Father shook his head. "No, I'm to deliver them personal, and see Mr. Leech himself. Tomorrow will do. I'll come back."

Twiss looked up at Father, his lips pursed. "As you will," he said, "but as it's from Sir Henry it'll be about the land grants in Canada, I expect?" His hand was still out.

Father seemed a little uncertain for a moment, then he said abruptly, "Why yes, it is." He tucked the letters back in his jacket, turned on his heel, and we went downstairs to the clatter on the Hard.

"Weasely little fellow that, Tom," he muttered, "altogether too big for his boots." Then: "You wait by Keppel's." He pointed out the inn sign a little way along the Hard. "The London coaches come in there. Your uncle should be in this afternoon. I'll find Will in the dockyard and we'll all have supper together — the Boar in Quay Road. We'll get lodgings there, too."

He was off and I was left to watch the bustle — wagons rumbling through the dockyard gates, carriages coming and going at the shops and at the inn, pedlars with their baskets and barrows calling their wares. A steam tugboat warped a tall sailing vessel down harbour. Smoke poured from its funnels. Its paddle wheels churned. The afternoon flew by. Shopkeepers put up their shutters and evening drew in.

The lamplighter had just started his rounds when the London coach clattered around the corner by the dockyard wall. There was Uncle Matthew, high up in front, the reins in his hands. He looked magnificent in his brown tail coat with yellow facings, white breeches, top boots and tall hat and his jaunty, pointed beard.

I ran beside, calling and waving and he saw me, grinned and whirled his whip in salute. The post-boy beside him raised his horn and let out a blast. Uncle Matthew cracked his whip and the horses dashed the last hundred yards. I raced after the coach and followed it into the big inn yard.

Uncle Matthew was down attending to his passengers and their boxes and the bags of mail. He had such a wide, warm smile — he was tall and straight and lively and so sure of himself. I watched him proudly until he was free.

"Tom lad, what brings you to wicked old Portsmouth? Up with you now." He tossed me up on the high seat, climbed up beside me. He handed me the reins and grinned. I shook them and we drove off to the stables and saw to the horses.

I told him what I could remember about the land grant. He let me run out of breath in my excitement and finally said: "Well, off to the Boar with you then, Tom. I'll follow along after I attend to things here and we'll hear all about it." He told me how to find Quay Road.

The narrow streets were crowded with clerks and shopgirls heading for home, labourers, soldiers and sailors, teamsters and tradesmen off to the taverns. Light streamed out of the open doorways, and voices — cheerful voices, growling voices, drunken voices — talked, laughed, sang.

An old beggar squatted, back to the wall, stumps of legs jutting out, holding out his cap: "Penny for old Jack Tar, mateys. Penny for old Jack Tar."

The signs of the inns and shops swinging overhead, the throngs of people, the lights and the sounds of the city around me all had a wonder and excitement about them I could never feel in

Edgeham. I envied Will — living with all this at his door. He had little time for me of course. His visits home were rare, and then he was usually chasing after the village girls.

The Boar was a big old inn close by the water near the harbour entrance, a gathering place mainly for soldiers, young and old. It was half full when I arrived and it had a rich smell of people, tobacco, boiled cabbage and strong drink. Potboys and serving girls carried mugs and trays to the scrubbed tables and the booths. The customers drank, laughed, talked, smoked, argued, filled the place with cheerful noise. I peered over heads and through the smoke, trying to find Father and Will, then searched through the back saloon and dining place without success.

There was Mr. Leech's clerk, though, sitting in a booth. He was half facing towards me and talking to someone across the table — two men, I thought, but I couldn't see around the high back of the seat they were in. One, at any rate, was a soldier. I could see the red sleeve and the buttons. The other man was completely hidden but I heard him laugh.

A potboy bumped into me, slopping ale out of the mugs he was carrying. He cursed and I slipped back to the main door just in time to see Father coming in with Will.

We found a table in a corner, and Father was ordering ale from the same surly potboy, when the door swung open and in burst Uncle Matthew. His tall hat was tipped over his eye, he wore a huge smile and he had two girls with him, one under each arm.

"Penny! Hey, Matthew Penny, you rogue!"

A grizzled corporal of the Royal Marines stood up at a neighbouring table and waved both arms. The men with him shouted their greetings too and Uncle Matthew danced the two giggling girls towards them through the crowded tables.

"Here you are, my beauties. My old friend, Corporal Miller and his gallant barrack-rats here will look after you — care for you like queens, they will — won't you Dusty? No — no, Dusty, I can't join you — sorry old friend, got business, family business, you know. Sit you down. Sit you down, now." Uncle Matthew pushed him back into his chair. "Brought these two little morsels along just for you Dusty, knowing you for a man of good taste, and seeing today is payday!"

He scooped one of the girls up in his arms and dropped her squealing and giggling right into Dusty's lap. The chair toppled over and down went the two of them, a tangle of legs, arms, skirts and petticoats.

The room exploded with cheers and laughter. Uncle Matthew stepped back, swept off his hat in a stately bow and strode quickly to our table.

He plunked his hat on my head, tapped it down over my ears and pulled up a chair.

"That'll teach him, Tom," he winked at me.

"The old blackguard owes me a packet. Little game of cards — a good month ago now. He keeps forgetting, he says. Those two frippets — they'll lead him a dance tonight. Poor old Dusty, he'll wake up tomorrow and wonder where his month's pay went. Next time, maybe, he'll pay me and be done with it. It'll cost him less!" Uncle Matthew laughed. Will laughed and so did I. Even Father smiled at him, shaking his head a little wryly.

"Same old Matthew," he said in his slow country voice. "Aren't you ever going to settle down?"

"Settle down?" Uncle Matthew's eyes widened. "Settle down? If you mean when am I going to stop having my bit o' fun, and when am I going to be an old sobersides like you, brother William," —he reached across the table, prodded Father's chest — "the answer is 'when I'm in my grave.'"

Father smiled back, still shaking his head, then he turned to me. "You know, Tom, when you're young you can't wait to be grown up, and when you're old you wish you were young again. Not Matthew though. He never did grow up."

"Oh, Father," Will leaped in. "You just envy him being off in London, and you stuck up there in the mud in Edgeham."

"There's more to life than roistering about, Will," said Father.

"Matthew doesn't just roister about, why he—"

Uncle Matthew broke in: "No cause to argue over me, you two. Come on now, let's have a drink and a bite o'food and you can tell me what young Tom here was jabbering about. Oho! Sal, me girl. Some service —"

Matthew got far better attention from Sal than Father had from the potboy. In no time we were tucking into steaming hot meat pies with potatoes, bread and cheese and washing it all down with the Boar's best brown ale.

"It's my payday today, too," Matthew said, "so eat up, you Edgeham Pennys. Uncle Matthew pays."

Father's mouth was full and he tried to protest, but Uncle Matthew cut him off. "Catch me while I have it in my pocket, William. No arguments now."

The talk turned to Canada and Father repeated most of the things the Admiral had said. I watched Uncle Matthew. He was frowning slightly, listening with half an ear, a little impatient. I held my breath. How I wanted to go, and how I wanted Uncle Matthew to be with us!

The dishes were cleared. Sal put a glass of rum in front of Uncle Matthew with a giggle. Father spread out the maps — and we crowded around.

The names were strange — English mixed with French. There was the "Grand River of the Ottawas," "The Great Falls of Chaudière," and at the far western side, running back from the shore of "Lac de la Chaudière" was a rectangular space marked "Onslow." It was blank. There were no roads, no towns, no churches — nothing marked on the land at all except straight lines and numbers showing the different lots. On the south side of the river was a space marked "Fitzroy."

Uncle Matthew pursed his lips. "So, William, we can have our pick of that, eh? Sight unseen. Hmm . . ." He beat a light tattoo on the table with his fingers.

"Well," he said, "if you want my opinion, that's the spot right there." He jabbed his finger at the map. "Look. 'Rapide des Chats.' Fast water, William — power for a mill. And there's a 'carrying place.' There'll be a road perhaps, and trade. A place for an inn, maybe. Right by the water — you can get produce to market, timber too."

"You only cut timber once, Matthew — you sow seed every year. Fast water means rocks. We need good soil. We should be further back, or down here."

"Ah! but can't you have it both ways? Each lot is 200 acres, mind. With two lots you'd have more land than the old Admiral." Matthew chuckled, warming to the idea a little. He downed his rum. Sal was there in a moment with another.

"Well, maybe that's the best place and maybe not," said Father. "The big thing is,

Matthew, are you for it? Will you come?"

"You know I'm not much of a farmer, don't you, William? Why, Tom here can plough straighter than I can. And I like the cities. So does young Will, eh? Village life suits you and Martha — and Tom too. He's like you. But me — I'm —"

Father spoke very seriously: "Tell me, Matthew, with all your running around and gambling, and your schemes for making money and the jobs you've had, what have you got now that you didn't have ten years ago?"

Matthew's mouth opened a little to make some retort. But he sat silent for a long time looking steadily back at Father. Then he looked at Will and then at me, and his eyes dropped.

"Nothing." He shook his head very slightly. "Just — nothing." I could barely hear him. "Thank you, William — for wanting your shiftless bachelor brother to come." He sat looking into his glass for a long moment, swirling the rum. Then he looked up at Father.

"How soon can we go?"

I caught my breath in delight.

Suddenly I felt someone near and I glanced up. It was Cornelius Twiss. He was standing near the table looking intently down at the map, and I had the feeling he had been there for some time.

He snorted a little and cleared his throat.

"Ah, Mr. Penny!" he said, smiling. "I happened to see you here and I thought I should bid you good evening and tell you that Mr. Leech will be in his chambers at four o'clock tomorrow afternoon." He stood there as though he rather expected to be asked to sit down with us.

Father turned in his chair, looked coldly at the shrivelled little man for a moment and said: "Thank you, Mr. Twiss. A good evening to you, sir."

They looked at each other in silence. The clerk's smile died, then he spun about and picked his way through the tables to the door.

Father watched him go. "Now what was he up to — being so friendly? This afternoon it was 'my good man.' Tonight, it's 'Mr. Penny.'"

"Oh, maybe he's just lonely, William," Matthew shrugged. "Poor little fellow. I'll wager he hasn't a friend in the world."

We turned back to our talk.

We were going to Canada — all of us. But when? How to pay for the passages? Will's apprenticeship — what to do about that? Our belongings — what to take?

At last it was all resolved. Uncle Matthew would go right away in the first available ship. He had a little money. It was spring now and he would get a fair start on the land before winter came. Father would sell everything we could not take and follow on with Mother and me.

Will, to his disappointment, would finish his apprenticeship and finally come to join us.

"It's the only way, Will," Uncle Matthew said.

"You're indentured and in another year you'll have your trade. Shipwrights will be needed out there — much more than here, I'll wager. There'll be real money in shipbuilding."

The noise in the inn grew around us, and we talked on and on, laying one plan upon another. Matthew kept calling for more drinks and quite outstripped Father who barely touched his, and Will who tried hard to keep up.

Excitement caught us all. Father's eyes shone as I had never seen them, and he spoke with a warmth I had never known. We were going. *We* were going. When Father said "we" he included me! Not just the boy who mucked out stables and fed the pigs and hoed potatoes and hauled water and lived in the same cottage. I was part of a grand and wondrous plan — a new life for the Pennys, for us all. I was Father's son. I mattered.

3. Darkness and Death

In the morning Uncle Matthew took Will with him to search for passages among the ships in harbour. I went with Father from shop to shop looking at everything — chairs and tables, tools and implements, harness, crockery, kettles, cutlery — everything we might need to take with us and all the sorts of things we might leave behind. He was pricing, not buying — working out how much we should get for this, how much we might pay for that. He tucked the facts in his mind and we moved on — from the brightest, cleanest shops down to the meanest, from the Hard to the back alley stalls and barrows.

Ordinarily I would have envied Will, being with Uncle Matthew, filled with his gaiety, laughing at his jokes. But today was different and Father was different, or perhaps I was different. We talked and talked as we had never talked before.

The four of us met at Mr. Leech's chambers as the guildhall clock struck four. Will and I were not really needed, so we headed off and explored the docksides. There was a great confusion of sailors and labourers working the ships, teamsters with their horses and drays, piles of produce, heaps of bales, great stacks of timbers — some coming, some going. We watched, ducked and dodged, pried and poked and peered — Will telling me about the ships and their rigging and how they were built and how they were sailed.

He was really friendly for once and quite happy to answer my questions. I had the feeling that he might even miss me. Indeed, he would be lonely when we were all gone, even though he would never admit it to anyone.

Will was tall and self-possessed and he had the same gaiety about him as Uncle Matthew. Everyone noticed it just as they said I was so like Father.

Will said: "Look Tom, that Indiaman warping in. Loaded with tea, I'll wager. Now that's what I'd do if I had some money — put it in cargoes. They make a packet, these merchants do. What would you do if you had money?"

Without a second thought I said: "Buy some land." Will smiled and shook his head.

* * *

Later, we sat in the evening sunshine at a table outside the Boar, waiting for Father and Uncle Matthew. The shadows darkened along the narrow street. The inn slowly filled with the evening trade. The lamps were lit, throwing deeper shadows across the laneways and a chill breeze whirled in from the harbour and brought the dank smell of the sea. I shivered a little.

24

"Will, where d'you suppose they are?"

"Oh, still at Mr. Leech's, I expect, or perhaps they're looking for a passage for Matt," said Will idly. "They'll be along. Got a penny, Tom?"

I nodded.

He said: "I've one. Two will buy a pint of ale. Come on — I'll give you half."

"No, Will." I was worried. "They shouldn't take this long. Let's go find them. Everyone's home from his work by now."

It was quite dark. The guildhall clock struck the hour — eight o'clock.

"I'm going to look — besides, I'm hungry."

"Oh, very well then," Will grumbled. "You cut along the docks, I'll go by the streets and we'll meet on the Hard in front of Number 4." He brightened. "Beat you there! Put the penny on it?"

"Right."

We were off. I dived down the covered laneway by the Boar and through a tangle of alleys to the docks. They were badly lit and strangely silent after the bustle of the day. I picked my way around the idle barrows and wagons, skirted the great stacks of goods. The ships alongside were quiet. Dim light glowed through skylights and scuttles and from occasional lanterns on deck.

There were few people about now. A watchman glowered at me suspiciously. Rats — big, black, ugly rats — scurried off, then watched with bright beady eyes as I passed. Blackness lay thick in the doorways and in the narrow alleys. A burst of muffled laughter rose and fell from a ship alongside. Silence then, except for my feet on the cobbles and the lap, slap, drip of water and the creaking of ships and rigging.

I moved as fast as I could, wary of my footing, glancing over my shoulder. The shadows seemed to whisper and move and reach out towards me.

"Ugh!" I tripped over a hawser and fell flat, half winded. I lay there, cursing at myself, nursing a bruised knee.

The noises of the town were far away. I could hear the water, and the rats, and the sound of my own breathing, and — something else? Something quite near — moving — a kind of clawing, sliding sound. A rasping noise. I crouched there, frozen. It was in the alley, in the darkness. I couldn't see, but there was something there. My heart stopped. Something — a low moan — no, someone. I couldn't run — I tried, but I couldn't. Someone was there, in the dark. In pain.

Another moan. I forced my feet towards the alley. The back of my neck crawled. Silence now, deadly silence. I hesitated a long moment, then stepped into the blackness, hands extended, groping, fearful.

"Who's there?"

Another step forward. Another. Another. My toe touched something and recoiled. Something soft there on the ground.

"Who — who is it?" I could just see him. I put my hand out. I could feel his body shudder.

He rasped: "Tom . . . Tom . . . "

My arms were around him holding him. Breath rattled in his throat.

"Knifed me, Tom . . . bad . . . Why, Tom? Why . . . ?" His voice trailed away.

"Who did Father, who?" I sobbed, my face close to his. I could see his mouth open struggling to breathe, his eyes nearly closed. They flickered an instant. He tried to speak, shook his head, shuddered again.

I raised him. Talked. Tried to lift him, to hold him. "Oh Father! What's happened? What's happened to you? Who . . . ?"

His head dropped back against my arm.

Tears blinded me. I tore to the dockside, shouting, shrieking, "Help, watch, murder! Help! My father! Help him! Help —"

I remember feet pounding, torches flaring, lanterns, men's faces in the gloom. Harsh voices, confusion. I remember my hands, sticky with blood.

The men moved quickly, lifted him.

"Easy, mates, easy — take 'im aboard the *Anne* there. Nearest ship."

Someone's arm lay across my shoulder. "Steady lad, steady as she goes. Ned's gone for the surgeon. We'll see to him now."

They carried him aboard and aft, eased him down a ladder and laid him on the bunk in a dim little cabin. I moved with them, in a dream, barely able to think.

"Bleedin' bad." They peeled off his jacket and shirt, started working over him. Blood welled up black from a deep wound high in his chest. I watched it as they mopped it, pressed a bandage over it. The blood soaked the bandage, trickled down his chest. The lantern flickered on his waxen face, on the heads of the sailors. The little ship creaked gently. Hawsers groaned, held her in against the tide. Blood seeped. The breathing of the silent men, feet sounding now on the deck above. The sailor's face turned up to me, lips tight, eyes grim, head slowly, slowly shaking.

My heart sank — a hollow agony in my chest. I watched his life ebb soundlessly away. He was gone.

Father was gone.

I had only just — found him. And he was gone.

4. A New Beginning

We buried Father in the churchyard in Edgeham. Mother and Will and Uncle Matthew, the old Admiral and our friends from the village. The sun shone on the old stone church. The daffodils nodded between the headstones. Birds sang their spring songs.

The vicar intoned the burial: " . . . ashes to ashes, dust to dust . . . " My heart ached in my chest. Why did it happen to us? We had everything ahead. Why, God, oh why did you do this to us?

Afterwards we four sat like lead in the kitchen. Questions lay between us — unasked, unanswered. Mother's arm lay tight across my shoulders. Her eyes were dry and sad.

Uncle Matthew stirred the fire with his good hand and stood staring into the coals. The other hand was bandaged and there was a long cut down his left cheek. He had been in some pain from a deep cut in his shoulder and badly battered ribs since the night Father died. He had been attacked as well, somewhere near the docks, around the time I had found Father.

He broke the silence.

"Martha, William was a real man. I mean — he and I often quarrelled. Brothers do. Used to say I should settle down — stop knocking around, save my wages. He was right, Martha. He was a good man. I mean really good and tough as oak. God knows why he was killed. It could have been the same ruffians as set on me. After purses, I suppose — any rate, they took everything I had. If we'd only been together —"

Silence choked the room.

He turned and faced Mother. "Martha, I've not got much, but what I have is yours. And I'll work to see that you and the boys have what you need. Everything will work out all right. You'll see." He smiled at us all. "Will you want to stay here, perhaps, and not go to Canada? It's very hard, you know."

There was a moment's silence.

"If you really want to go, though," he went on, "I'll make ready ahead of you as best I can as we planned. I have an offer to work my passage."

Mother frowned a little seeking a reply.

A knock at the door. The vicar and the Admiral came in. They quietly offered words of comfort.

"And, Mrs. Penny," the Admiral finished, "you're to stay here and not mind about the rent until you decide what to do — you and your boys."

Mother sat very straight. She looked around the kitchen — her kitchen for as long as I could remember. Then she spoke, gently and firmly. "William wanted us to emigrate, Sir Henry. We have his land to go to. We must do as he would wish. Matthew Penny has agreed to go ahead and prepare the way. Tom and I will go when we have settled up here and have saved our passage money. Will stays at the dockyard 'til his time is served. Then I hope he will join us too."

She stood and raised her head. Tears glistened in the corners of her eyes. "Sir Henry, I must thank you for your kindness. This has been a happy home. We had little but each other and we wanted no more. But William would have gone — for the sake of the boys. And so must I."

"Madam," he said gravely, "your husband would be proud of you. The decision is yours, and you have made it well. You Pennys will find the home and the happiness you deserve."

He paused for a moment and cleared his throat. "I have an acquaintance in Montréal," he continued. "A Scotsman in the fur trade. A Mr. Jamie MacPherson. He could be helpful to you. He can be found at Beaver Hall when he is not off adventuring. I will give you a letter to him before you leave."

He took her hand then and bowed low over it just as though she were a great lady. He turned to Uncle Matthew.

"A word, if I may, Penny, and with young Tom here." He bowed again to Mother and led the way outside. We followed him into the sun.

He cleared his throat. "Difficult time to be asking questions, Penny, but I'm Magistrate here as you know. Your brother lived in this parish and I must satisfy myself regarding his death. I hope we can find some evidence to lay the murdering devils by the heels."

Uncle Matthew nodded.

"Now, young Tom here found his father about eight o'clock?"

"Yes sir," I said. "It was dark about half an hour and Will and me — I — heard it strike eight just before."

"Where were you then, Penny?"

"Why, I stayed at Mr. Leech's chambers, sir, while his clerk wrote out the papers — the deeds and so on. We had discussed it all — William and Mr. Leech and me — and settled on our lots, and signed the papers. Mr. Leech left. But there was the description of the land to write, so I stayed behind with the clerk. William left for the Boar, to see the boys got some dinner."

"How long did you stay on?"

"Oh, about an hour, I suppose, sir. He seemed to take great pains and write very carefully."

"Then you were set upon too? By the docks?"

"That's right, sir. Came at me in a rush. Two of them at least. I've no idea how long I was out."

"Would you recognize them?"

"Not a chance, sir." Matthew shook his head.

The Admiral grunted and turned to me, his tufted white eyebrows pulled together. I told him how I had heard sounds in the alley and found Father nearly gone, and how the sailors had carried him aboard the ship.

He said: "Tom now, did you see anyone?"

The dreadful scene came back. I couldn't speak. I could only shake my head. He put his hand on my shoulder and spoke very gently.

"Did you hear anything? Did you spot anything at all that would give you any ideas? Anything strange?"

I fought back the tears that burned behind my eyes.

"No sir," I breathed.

"Cutpurses!" The Admiral turned to Matthew with an angry snort. "Getting worse every day. Well, there's no more evidence you or Tom could give even if we did catch them. Nothing to hold you back then, Penny." He put out his hand. "And the very best of good fortune to you."

* * *

A week after, on a showery, gloomy afternoon, came a strange visit. Mr. Cornelius Twiss arrived at our door. He was wearing his worn black suit and a black stock and he stood in the kitchen shaking the drops of water off his tall black hat. He looked like a small, sad, hunched blackbird drying itself after the rain. He spoke mournfully and at length to Mother, expressing his sympathy and urging her to be thankful for her fine children and for living in such a pleasant cottage in a peaceful village.

Mother offered tea and a chair and after

settling down Mr. Twiss cleared his throat noisily.

"Now, Mrs. Penny," he said. "I did wish to spare you the pain of discussing this matter. However, after attempting to find your good brother-in-law, I at last discovered he had left very abruptly two days ago. Very hastily, it seems, and indeed he has with him all the papers which establish his and your late husband's claims to their chosen lots of land — in Onslow Township, I believe it is.

"As I understand it, Mrs. Penny, a landholder must build some sort of dwelling or farm building on his lot within a year in order to secure his title. All of this, of course, must be legally put in order in the colony itself.

"They tell me," he sniffed, and took a long suck at his cup of tea, holding the saucer right up under his chin and crooking his little finger, "they tell me, madam, that they have legal registry offices and even a semblance of courts of law. Although who in his right mind would wish to go there to practice a profession — with, of course," he cleared his throat noisily, "due respect to Mr. Penny and your late husband. Having both been military men, I suppose they are somewhat more adventuresome than most — and somewhat more inclined to take what one might call — ah — a long shot, I daresay."

He downed his tea and dabbed his lips with a rather dirty pocket handkerchief which he kept up his sleeve.

"Now madam, I must advise you that Mr. Matthew Penny also has papers which allow him legal title to your lot of land — as well as to his own — in the event of your husband's death." He emphasized these last words as though underlining them in a legal document. He went on: "The two brothers took into account the hazards of going to the colonies — the ocean passage, the terrible cold, the smallpox: and now I understand the cholera is rife in Québec where the emigrant ships land. They decided to pool their land, so to speak. Of course, it was understood between them if aught should happen to your husband, then Matthew Penny would look after the interests of you and your children. If Matthew Penny were to die now, of course, all the land would fall to you."

Mother said: "Thank you, Mr. Twiss. I did not know of this. It sets my mind at rest to know that Matthew can protect our interests and our land title until we arrive. My William was a prudent man." She was biting her lip and very close to tears.

Mr. Twiss cleared his throat again. "Well — ah madam. It was, in fact, Matthew Penny's notion — but no matter, the fact remains that your land is legally in his hands. I must advise you that you will probably have to depend on his goodwill rather than on any legal obligation on his part."

Mother's face stiffened and she leaned across the table towards the little blackbird of a man. "Mr. Twiss," she said evenly, "I do not truly understand your legal talk, but I believe you are saying that my brother-in-law, Matthew, might cheat me and my children. I say to you that whatever happens, Matthew would do no such thing. He will do as my husband would have wished. Some say that Matthew is harum-scarum. I can tell you, Mr. Twiss — he is an honest man and he will do his best for us." Her face flushed and she sat back in her chair.

"And pray, Mr. Twiss, why have you come all the way to Edgeham to tell me this?"

"Dear madam, pray forgive me for giving a quite uncalled-for impression. I do hope I have not offended." The little clerk fumbled for his handkerchief and blew his nose in confusion.

"I have, in fact, come," he said at last, "on behalf of — ah — a certain party, to offer you a handsome sum for your rights to this land in Canada. This person has a fancy for the location to carry on some form of business. Having no rights as an old soldier or sailor himself, he is prepared to pay you £500 and a like amount to Matthew Penny for the two lots. Five hundred pounds, madam. I have papers ready and a bank draft with me." He patted his pocket and leaned across the table. "Imagine! You could buy this cottage for your own from the landlord and have plenty left to bring up young Tom here the way your husband would have wished. You could all stay here in Edgeham — he could go to school, I daresay —"

Mother stood up abruptly. Her chair scraped back over the stone floor. "I know what my husband would have wished, Mr. Twiss." Her voice shook. "My husband made up his mind we should go and go we shall —"

She stood straight and still. Tears shone in her eyes. She looked directly at him and he turned his eyes away.

"— even though, Mr. Twiss — even though I leave my heart behind with him in Edgeham churchyard." Her voice broke. She almost whispered: "There is no more to say."

There was a long hush. The kettle breathed and I could hear rain pattering gently outside. The kitchen was dark now and chill.

Mr. Twiss sat with pursed lips, staring at Mother. Then he coughed, rose and backed away from the table, hands clasped in front, bowing from the waist. He muttered goodbye and his compliments.

"Should you reconsider —" he said, then shook his head as though in wonder.

I handed him his hat, opened the door and walked out with him to the gate through the soft spring rain. I opened it dumbly.

He turned to me quickly, hissed, "Think on it boy. Why d'you suppose your Uncle Matthew sailed off in such a hurry, eh?" His hand darted to my shoulder, clawlike, gripped me to the bone. I tried to pull back but he held me fast. His face moved close to mine. His lips barely moved.

"With your father dead he saw a chance to grab your land as well as his own. That's why. And he can do it. If you and your Mother get out there you'll find you have nothing. You hear? Nothing!"

He stopped. I could hear his breath between his teeth.

"You've got a head, Tom. Use it. Talk to your Mother. Take the £500. Live here in peace. Forget Canada and forget your uncle." He spat out the words. "He's worthless."

His eyes held mine for a long moment and his fingers bit my shoulder. Then he turned sharply away and bobbed down the lane towards the inn.

He was wrong about Uncle Matthew. I knew it. He'd never steal from anyone. But £500 for a piece of land we'd never seen? What would Uncle Matthew have done if Twiss had offered that much money to him before he left? Would he have taken it? Given up the land?

I thought of Uncle Matthew at the Boar — his laughter and his banter, his easy way with people and with money. Easy come, easy go. He liked money. No doubt of that. He liked spending it. He wasn't a farmer. What would he have done? What *would* he have done?

* * *

Six weeks dragged by. Primroses brightened the ditches. Linnets nested in the hedge and filled the yard with song. Swallows swooped beneath the eaves and the fields greened with new-grown grass. But there was no joy for us. They were weeks of sadness for Mother, of nagging doubts for me.

Then one sparkling day in June came a letter from the Admiral. Mr. Leech had found a free passage for us. We would have to work our way. Mother would look after the ration book and provision stores. I would work in the galley helping the cook. It would cost us nothing. We could leave in a week's time. Doubts, fears and worries disappeared in the excitement and haste of getting ready. We were going. Going to Canada. Going to our new home. Our own farm. Our new land.

The morning we left Edgeham, Mother and I knelt by Father's graveside, one last time. I said a prayer to myself for him, for Mother and for all of us. We were leaving now, leaving this forever, going to an empty square on a strange map of a wild and distant land.

A skylark sang its lone clear song. Our journey had begun.

5. Dirk Black

The brigantine Southdown, out of Portsmouth, bound for Québec, loaded with emigrants! The gentle green of England faded and we were alone on the vast sea. Alone and sailing westward.

"Four weeks passage, with luck and a fair wind," said Barnaby, the wooden-legged cook, "and God bless them good folk jammed in below decks when she starts to blow."

It was a whole new world, the ship and the sea. And it was a happy time. Barnaby never stopped talking, telling me, showing me. I scrubbed, I cleaned, I fetched bucket upon bucket of coal. I stoked the galley fire. I peeled potatoes, I carried the fannies full of Barnaby's dreadful stew, his water-thin soup to the fo'c's'le for the crew's dinners. I dodged the good-natured abuse of the seamen; kept well away from hard-eyed Captain Bardwell, and from Mr. Soulby and Dirk Black, the bosun's mate. Admiral Hardcastle had done us a real service in arranging our passages, but no favourites were played in Captain Bardwell's ship and they made sure we knew it.

The voyage wore on. The ship heaved and

pitched and pounded to windward. Coming back from Québec she would be loaded deep with timber, but now she was light and tender. The rolling, wet, slippery deck kept most of the passengers huddled below in their reeking, creaking quarters, all the more miserable because they had nothing to do. As Barnaby said: "Less work for us in the galley, mate!"

One bell in the first dogwatch — half-past four in the afternoon. Barnaby and I took our half-hour spell from the galley. We sat on deck, our backs against the fo'c's'le hatch watching the bowsprit rear up to the lead-grey sky then point down into the waves 'til the dolphin-striker cut the water. Southdown lifted up and over the long Atlantic swells, up and over the long Atlantic swells, up and over. Timbers creaking, canvas crackling, the wind humming in the shrouds. Again and again the sea surged and sounded under her bow, creamed up through the hawse and ran aft in the scuppers.

Ding-ding!

"Two bells, me lads."

It was Dirk Black, the bosun's mate. His voice came right on the heels of the ship's bell. I hadn't heard him, but then he was a man who moved quickly and lightly — like a cat almost — heavy set as he was.

"You'll be getting back to work now, Barnaby, having spent your stand-easy and a bit more a-filling up o' young Tom's head there with a lot o' nonsense, no doubt." He winked at me and we scrambled up.

"A bird whispered that the Captain, bless his heart, is minded to make his rounds tomorrow forenoon. So you-lot best get busy a-scrubbing out and squaring away that so-called galley o' yours. Looks more like the hold in a Portugee fishing schooner. And Tom — you can bring me down a fanny o' tea. Now." The word snapped out like the crack of a whip: "Move!"

Move we did.

* * *

Dirk Black ran the fo'c's'le navy style, so the hands said. Everyone had his place, and there was a certain place for everything, and first choice went to the senior hand — the bosun's mate. Some of them grumbled, but never in Dirk Black's hearing. They were all wary of him. His eyes were always on the move under their heavy black eyebrows, and his mood could change in a flash. Still, he was fair enough with me, and pretty attentive to Mother, in a way.

I carried the fanny forward along the pitching deck, down the fo'c's'le hatch and aft to the bosun's mate's curtained-off corner. He was sitting at the table writing slowly with a stub of lead pencil.

He glanced up. "Set her down, Tom, and get us a couple o' mugs over there. That's a good fellow."

I poured two mugs of tea and stood watching

him finish his writing. He had huge hands, tufted with black hair. They were calloused and scarred and the third finger was missing from the one that held the pencil. Working with cables and rigging, splicing, reefing, heaving and hauling took their toll of a sailor over the years.

"Sit ye down, Tom, sit ye down and drink up. Time to have a bit of a yarn with old Dirk. Not as old as Barnaby, mind. That rascal went to sea in Noah's Ark." He took a pull at his mug.

"Well, what's taking you to Onslow Township, lad?"

I told him about our land and about Uncle Matthew going on ahead. "You see," I hesitated, "my father — died — and we're going to farm the land together — Uncle Matthew and Mother and me —"

"Sorry, Tom — about your father," his voice was quiet, "but you'll do well. Your Uncle Matthew now — will he be meeting you in Québec?"

I shook my head. "There was no ship leaving ahead of the Southdown to take a letter. Besides it's a long way, I think."

"You know," he said, "I was once minded to take up some land." His eyes looked a little wistful. "Good to have a family, Tom. Sailors don't have that kind o' luck, though. Still — well, look here now. You should learn a bit more about sailoring. You give me a hand now and then, up on deck. I'll show you how to splice and make sail and all. Fact is, I have to rig a new footrope up aloft on the fore top-gallant tomorrow. Me regular mate, 'e's got the boils or some such. On light duty. You'll give me a hand then, eh Tom?"

I hesitated a moment, "I — I'll have to ask Barnaby."

"No lad. You *tell* Barnaby that the bosun's mate needs you. Time that old skate peeled the spuds hisself." He winked.

I found Mother on the fo'c's'le later, and told her about the next day's excitement. Dirk Black came forward checking rigging, casting his quick eye here, testing a lashing with his foot there. He was brushed and shaved and neat, wearing clean white trousers and a short blue jacket.

"Ah, Mrs. Penny! A pleasant evening," he smiled, "Can I join you two for a spell?"

"Why, yes indeed, Mr. Black. Tom tells me you're going to turn him into a sailor."

"Aye! Learns fast, does Tom. Do him a bit o' good. Even if he is going to be a farmer." He fished through his pockets. "Tom lad, just nip down to my mess, would you? You'll find my pipe setting on the locker there."

Off I went.

No pipe on the locker though, or on any of the sills, or tucked on top of the beam where Dirk Black slung his hammock. I opened the locker. No pipes in there. His sea chest was lashed in a corner, locked. Finally, I climbed the ladder back to the fo'c's'le.

Dirk Black was sitting on the hatch next to

Mother, talking, nodding his head — very close to her. My heart gave an odd lurch.

He looked up. "Oh! Thank 'e, Tom. But here I am with my pipe tucked in my belt all the time. Forget my own head next!" He was smiling. Mother looked at her hands in her lap.

I crawled into my hammock that night feeling empty and lonely, thinking back on Father and Edgeham. Now Mother and Dirk Black ran through my mind. I barely slept.

* * *

The morning watchman shook me well before dawn as usual, in time for me to stir the galley fire, make tea for the mate who stood the morning watch, and heat up the Captain's shaving water.

I rolled out and stood limp, half awake, feeling the deck shifting, hearing the groaning of the ship.

I groped my way on deck, and stood there numbed and cold, shaking off sleep. The ship was wrapped in fog. It seemed to press in on my eyes and its chill fingers crept inside my clothes. Water dripped from the rigging. It was oddly silent. The wind and the fog seemed to muffle and deaden the ship's usual sounds.

I strained my eyes aft. I could just see the dark loom of the mainmast, but there was no sign of the friendly binnacle light through the gloom.

The galley was in the deckhouse amidships, and I bumbled aft towards it. Perhaps Mother would be there getting herself an early cup of tea as she often did.

A light shone weakly through the fog from the galley scuttle. I reached the deckhouse, ran my hand wetly along it, hearing a murmur of voices.

Mother's, yes. Mother's voice — then the deeper voice of a man. I drew closer and I could make out his words.

"— You're a very handsome woman now, Mrs. Penny —"

Silence. I stopped, with my hand on the door latch.

"Mr. Black, kindly keep your hands to yourself. It's one thing to pass a friendly time of day. It's another —"

"Now, now, now. You just be nice to Dirk, Mrs. Penny — Martha, eh? That's it — Martha. It's a long voyage and — you just look after Dirk and Dirk'll —"

I stood there, uncertain.

Mother's voice, cool and firm, "Mr. Black, that's enough!" There was a scuffling sound.

I tugged open the door to see Mother catch Dirk Black a clout across the face. He stood there a moment, his hand up to his cheek, and then he leaped at her, and I went for him. He heard me, whirled, caught me with the back of his hand, and sent me flying across the galley. I clattered in among the coal scuttles on my back and he stood looking down at me with his lips pressed tight and his eyes glittering.

Then he turned to Mother again. I pulled myself up and charged, fists swinging blindly.

He cursed, picked me up like a sack of flour. One hand took me by the throat and I could hear him growl. His face was close to mine, twisted with rage, and his eyes burned into me. His hand tightened. Breath caught in my throat —

Then suddenly it was over. The snarl disappeared. His grip relaxed. He set me on my feet. He blinked and pulled his mouth into a smile, gave a short laugh.

"Good morning to you, Tom. You didn't take me serious now, did you? Just having a friendly little talk we was — me and your mother. You startled me, coming up from behind like that, I must say."

He turned to Mother. "No offence, Mrs. Penny. A little carried away, I was. Forgot my manners. You can't blame a sailorman for being taken with you, now can you?"

"Please, Mr. Black," Mother said coldly, "don't forget yourself again."

He winked at me, said "See you on the fo'c's'le at four bells, Tom," and he left just as though nothing had happened. I felt my throat. It had all happened so quickly, but it had happened. For a moment I was sure he was going to kill me. And now . . .

I looked up at Mother. She shrugged, clasped her hands in front of her and stood looking down at them. Without raising her eyes she said: "I think Tom, we had best just forget about this."

The lamp swung slowly with the ship, shifting the shadows on Mother's face. The banked-up fire popped gently. She stood there, her eyes down, not moving. My heart thumped slow and hard against my chest. Dirk Black's smile and wink — and I could still feel his fingers on my throat. I didn't understand. I really didn't understand. I only knew that I had felt a hair away from death a moment ago — that there was danger for the two of us. And I knew that nothing in the world would drag me up into the rigging with Dirk Black.

When four bells rang I stayed in the galley and Dirk Black sent no word.

We bore on, silent through the fog, the next day a gray extension of the night.

I watched for Black. Every waking minute, I watched for him. The strange feeling grew that he could see me, that he could see through the bulkheads, through the clinging fog, that he was watching me. But I didn't see him anywhere, and I was afraid to ask.

After dark, there was nothing you could fix your eye to on deck, and moving about was like walking in a dream. That evening, I worked my way forward along the lee side, keeping one hand on the bulwarks, moving my feet carefully.

The ship ghosted along, shrouded, smothered in the fog. I could barely make out the surface of the sea. Then I heard the strangest sound . . . a bird . . . yes, it was a bird. Not a gull though. It was chirping. A sparrow sound — one I hadn't heard for weeks.

I moved softly on a step or two, and there it was, right by my hand on the bulwark. Yes. A sparrow. A grayish, streaked sort of sparrow as nearly as I could see. But so far from land? It must be completely exhausted. It eyed me warily. I moved very gently and took it in my hand. It scarcely moved. It sat there helpless, on my palm, staring at me with its tiny beady eye. A sparrow. I could warm it up, feed it a little. Perhaps . . .

A hand closed over mine — a huge hand. It enclosed the bird, all but the tiny head, and held it there in front of me. The hand was missing a finger.

I turned. Looming over me, his great shoulders hunched, his chin somehow pulled down onto his chest, was Dirk Black. Those eyes of his glittered again as they had in the galley. They bored into me. And inches from my face, in his great fist, the wretched little sparrow moved slightly, trapped and helpless. It seemed to plead with me.

I was rooted, held by the sparrow, by Dirk Black's eyes, by a horror of the man.

"Now, Tom Penny," he breathed.

I tried to cry out. But no sound came. We were alone, we two, wrapped in the fog. And between us his fist and the bird.

His voice came again with a whiff of rum. "No one! No one this side o' the gates o' hell — or beyond — man, woman or boy — crosses Dirk Black's bows. No one." His words were slurred a little. "And Dirk Black never forgets."

His face drew down even closer. I could see the whites of his eyes, the heavy eyebrows, gleaming teeth, lips pulled back like some beast.

"Dirk Black never forgets. Maybe it's now, Tom. Maybe later. But you'll never get to Onslow. Never get to farm that land. I'll have it, ye hear? I'll snuff you out —" His voice was a low snarl. "In my own good time, Tom, I'll snuff you out. Just —" he raised his fist a little, "like —" It bunched around the sparrow, tightened slowly, slowly, slowly —

"That!"

A slight crack. The bird jerked once. He slowly opened his fist and it trembled its tiny life away and lay there quite still, a crumpled heap of feathers. The sight of it held me fixed in dread. I stood there — how long?

Some shift of the deck, some sound, broke the spell. I stepped back, turned. He reached for me and cursed. I heard him scramble. I ran blindly, then caught my foot and fell. I shrank against the bulwark listening. There were a thousand things on deck to trip over. Dirk Black knew them like his own hand.

His breathing. I could hear it. Was that him

looming in the fog? I held my breath, crouched, waiting. No sound now.

The fo'c's'le hatch. It could only be fifteen paces away. Was that its glimmer of light?

Silence. No movement now. Where was he? Close. Waiting for me to move, then — the ship lifted uneasily. A block thumped up forward. Silence again. My breath was running out.

The fog had thinned a little. I could see the foremast now. My breath burst out in a rush and I leaped for it, ran, ducked behind it, tried to hold silent. I was quivering, the breath catching in my throat. He heard me.

Something loomed in the fog. I whirled, dashed for the hatch, tripped, rolled, scrambled, clawed at something — someone. It was —

"Steady matey, steady. What's up with you?" Barnaby! Oh, it was Barnaby. I couldn't speak. I had just broken out of a dreadful dream — surely it was a dream.

"Crashing around the upper deck like that —"

I looked over my shoulder, gulping air.

"What're you puffing about, Tom? Sit down now. You're shaking like a ship in irons." His hand was on my shoulder.

"Black," I gasped. "Dirk Black — he — he —"

"He what?"

I tried to say it, that he'd threatened to kill me — some day. He'd killed the sparrow. He was going to kill me — he's killed the sparrow.

"Sparrow," I gabbled, "sparrow. Sparrow on deck. He — he killed it — he —"

"Sparrow, you say? There you are. There's sparrows on Sable Island. Reckoned we must be nigh on in soundings by now. I came up for a sniff o' the wind. I figured —"

I looked aft. The fog had thinned a bit. There was the binacle light. No sign of Black. I couldn't stop trembling.

" . . . no sky for days." Barnaby rattled on.

I was getting a hold on myself now.

"Doubt the Captain knows our position too good. Really should have a lookout posted here. Well, if he'd just asked old Barnaby for advice — sparrow, eh?"

I got my breath back.

"Barnaby," I sobbed, "Barnaby. He's going to kill me — he swore — he —"

"Hush!" He slapped his hand over my mouth. He wouldn't listen.

He sniffed. His eyes strained through the fog.

"By God! There's —"

He turned his head slowly, listening.

"Feel it?" he whispered. "Listen!" The deck seemed to rise and fall a little more sharply under my feet. I strained my ears, held my breath. A low, growling, rumbling sounded behind the ship noises. It faded away, and there was nothing. Was that it again?

I turned to Barnaby, tugged his arm, pleading, "Barnaby —"

He shook me off sharply, stabbed his finger through the fog.

"There — breakers! Shoalwater!"

A smudgy white, broken line loomed, almost glowed, through the fog from the port bow to right ahead.

Barnaby faced aft and roared: "Breakers ahead — port bow!" To me: "Tom! At the double! To the mate — he's on watch. Tell him! Then tell the Captain."

I raced aft, Black forgotten. Barnaby's voice behind me at the fo'c's'le hatch bellowed: "All hands on deck! Stations to wear ship. Move yourselves, lads — double quick. Breakers —"

The mate was gaping forward. I stammered, breathless: "Breakers — surf ahead — port bow, sir. I'll tell the Captain."

I heard the mate shout: "Hard over! All hands on deck."

I dived for the after hatch and tumbled down, dashed to the farthest door, thumped on it, threw it open. It was pitch dark.

I shouted: "Captain, sir. Breakers ahead —!"

The ship lurched, rolled heavily over to port. I fell in a heap inside the door. A grunt and an oath from the Captain. He ran right over me, thundered up the ladder. Feet thumped on deck.

Another lurch — heavier. A crash. An enormous shuddering blow. Shouts above.

I was at the ladder. The ship groaned, lifted under me, plunged downward, shuddered again, then lay right over on her port side. I fell hard against the bulkhead, struggled back to the ladder. I clung, tried desperately to pull myself up. Water rushed down the hatchway, swept me from the ladder. I fought back as the stern lifted again. Somehow I clawed my way up and through the hatch.

The ship lay right over to port, lifting and pounding — lifting and pounding. Surf hissed by under the stern. The roar of breakers filled my ears. Waves crashed in over the starboard bulwarks and swept across the decks. We were hard around. I clung to the hatch. Shouts, screams of women forward. I must get to Mother!

A cry: "Tom!" Was it? Was it her? A wave broke over me.

A rending, tearing crash. The mainmast toppled over to port. There was the helmsman clinging to the wheel, waist deep in water. Helpless! He swept away. The wheel spun wildly. I gulped for air and clung for my life.

Another wave. The hatch shuddered and shifted. I was nearly torn away. A rope slashed across my face. I clutched it, knotted it somehow around me. A huge wave towered up, up and roared down. Another — another! The hatch splintered, cracked loose. It slid down the crazy slant of the deck, dragged me with it. It hung up on the bulwarks. White raging water tore at me, battered me. A wave surged up under the hatch and tossed it clear. The rope held me to it. I struggled to swim, lungs bursting.

Black, white, tumbling, frothing water flung me up for an instant. I took one gasp of air, spun down again, clinging to the hatch, then surged up, lifted high on a crest.

For a moment I could see the dim form of the ship, white water surging over her. Cries came faint in the dark, through the crash of surf. I whirled down again, then up — dragged by the rope.

I tried to get clear — get back to the wreck — get back to Mother. My fingers picked at the rope around my waist.

The knot was jammed, the other end was secured somewhere under water. I tried to find it, my fingers numb, helpless. I dived under into the blackness — once, twice. No use.

Where was the ship now? My stomach heaved, turned, heaved again, threw up sea water. I clung, retching helplessly. My hatch and the waves swept me on.

It was quieter now, and darker. Fog. Silence. And the cold. I could feel its grip. My strength was drained away. All I could do was hold to my hatch and pray . . .

Mother, the ship — the sea. The sea would have us all.

6. *Rosie and Elen*

Ship noises — creaking, heaving — a dim light. Some sort of feeling, hearing, understanding crept back to me. I was dreaming. Lying in bed, warm — warm and dry. Perhaps I was alive. I drifted away . . .

* * *

A quiet voice said: "How's it feel, lad?"

I couldn't reply. Yes, they were ship noises. I was alive . . .

I tried to speak. My lips were swollen, cracked, rough to my tongue. At last I asked him. Had he found anyone? Anyone else?

"One man, lad. One other along of you. Has a leg broke. No," he said, "no. He hasn't got a wooden one. He's in poor shape, too."

Mother gone, and Barnaby. Mother and Barnaby — gone with the rest. My heart sank in an empty sea. I was alone.

Only sleep took away the desolation.

* * *

Little by little I grew stronger, felt life return. My hopelessness ebbed. The tiny cabin was safety and warmth. The quiet voice urged me on. I began to wish for the light of day.

He said: "You'll be on deck in no time now, me lad. Try a drop o' this stew."

My loss was still there, a deep and empty void.

* * *

I sat wrapped in a blanket in a sheltered corner by the taffrail of the *Rosie and Elen* — schooner, out of St. John's, Newfoundland. The August sun shone bright and warm. The schooner slipped briskly along, heeled well over to a fresh, clean sou'westerly breeze. I was alive and well and I had just begun to really believe it!

Paddy — Captain Paddy Isnor — perched near me, his hand on the wheel. He had a stubbly, blackish, greyish beard and a brown face. His beak of a nose and his hooked chin seemed almost to meet. He was always smiling. He had crinkled, wrinkly, darting eyes — bright as a bird's.

His glance flicked up to the luff of the mainsail, checking its set, then darted off to windward, gauging the wind and sea, forward around the horizon, then inboard, checking the rigging and the deck cargo — a glance at the compass, then off on the rounds again. He always hummed — or sang — one of his Newfoundland songs. I could barely understand the words.

Rosie and Elen — Captain Paddy Isnor, Master — bound for Québec with a cargo of molasses and rum, had very nearly run me under in the fog somewhere northwest of Sable Island.

Paddy said I'd been so near death they'd almost stitched me up in a hammock, soaking wet, and dropped me straight back in the sea.

"Oh! We'd have read the prayers proper like. Better than drowning all on your own, you know. Mind, I was giving you the benefit of the doubt like, seeing as I'd no way to tell if you was Protestant or Catholic —"

He looked down at me wedged in my corner. "Tom, me boy" — he said "bye" — "Tom, it's time to start earning your passage. You're eating nigh a man's rations. Got some colour to you. Not looking that bad at all at all. You take the wheel. Old Paddy'll learn you to steer his darlin' *Rosie* here while he lights a pipe."

Rosie and Elen lifted and plunged. I felt the wheel tug under my hand and the sun and the wind on my face. It was good to be alive.

"Yes sir, Tom," he mused, "more unwary ships than you care to think about — and some wary ones too — has clewed up on Sable. If I had just a mite of all their cargo, I'd be rich. Sable's no good for honest wreckin', though. Not like some of your fine old spots in Newfoundland — like Cape Pine, say. And there's a rescue station on Sable, too. Doubt, though, they'd find any of your people. Reckon your ship," he said, "must o' just hung up on the nort' end. You must o' washed over the shoals like and drifted nor'west on your hatch cover. Wonderful lucky you was — not like some, eh?"

I looked away quickly. Why? — oh why?

He said softly: "Sorry, me son, sorry. That's how it is when folk goes to sea, you know. After we picked you up we searched all the rest of the day. Felt right in to the lee side of Sable, we did. Not a sign, 'cepting for the big sailor with the leg broke. No, no Tom, he didn't see anyone else — least as far as I can make out. He's tucked away up for'ard. You can speak to him 'bout it when he's able. A few days yet. He's still wonderful poorly. Number's up, it's up — and that's it. Yours ain't up — not yet it ain't. You're a tough one for an Englishman!"

He clapped me on the shoulder. "Live hearty, lad. You can stay along of us if you like. Look, we got a fine cargo aboard! Make a tidy bit on it in Québec!"

He took his pipe from his mouth and spat clear over the lee rail. "Now, I don't go much on your Canadians, most of them leastways. Don't hardly understand their talk, I don't. Sooner trade with them Yankees in the Boston States. Still and all, there's a dollar or three to be made in Québec — and I got me some special friends there, too!"

He winked.

"Watch your luff there, Tom. Bear up, no up, up on your helm a wee! Home did you say? Home? No, old *Rosie* here's home. Stay in Newfoundland, Tom, and you starve. You borrows from the merchants to outfit your ship for to fish.

Then they takes the fish and calls their own price for it. All in cahoots they are. Never pays you enough for next season's rigging out. So pretty soon they owns your ship and your dories and your gear. In the end they owns you — and your wife, too."

He spat again and looked away at the horizon for a long time. It was sharp and clear and cloudless, off there to the north. His face seemed to shrivel and tighten, thinking of the past.

"We been starved by the French, flogged to ribbons by them English admirals. Now it's the merchants — English too. They're squeezing what's left, Tom. Squeezing."

He lay silent a while. Then he turned and grinned suddenly and whacked me on the shoulder.

"But Paddy Isnor's not going to let hisself be split like a codfish and flaked out to dry. No sir. Dollars for Jamaica molasses and rum in Québec beats pennies for fish in Newfoundland. Me and the b'ys does all right. Tom. It's shares for pay and some fun at the end of each v'yage. There's naught keeps a good man down." He slapped a hand on the wheel. "Nor a good ship!"

I liked Captain Paddy. I liked "the b'ys." Billy, the mate — "the young feller" — with his red hair and freckled face and bow legs — quick as a cat and muscles of iron. No teeth in front!

"Lost 'em in Boston. Terrible sad," he told me.

"Can't play me Jew's harp no more. I give it to Eldon."

Eldon was a quiet, solemn, older fellow — short like Paddy and Billy, but thicker in body and slower about the ship. He took his watch and he tended the galley. Paddy claimed Eldon's "fish-and-brewis" — a mess of salt cod and ship's biscuit and pork — was "the best this side of Port aux Basques — which ain't saying much."

Zekiel was huge. He could have tucked his three shipmates under one arm and still have room for me and Prince William, the cat. He was black — the first black man I'd ever seen. He frightened me at first, then puzzled me.

That evening at supper he eyed me quietly, then said, "Look Tom." He laid his huge forearm on the table beside mine. "It won't rub off — you jus' try." He smiled and his teeth gleamed white.

Zekiel found some duck and stitched me up a pair of trousers and a bag for my kit. Eldon had an old striped flannel sailor's shirt which he cut down to fit me and someone produced a battered, peaked cap.

"Proper sailor." Paddy nodded with approval.

Good shipmates. Good ship.

We surged along up the gulf, running before a strengthening sou'easterly. The wind backed to east, then nor'east and stronger, driving in the rain. Huge, rolling, gray, white-streaked waves piled up. We shortened sail; *Rosie and Elen* roared along, surging, hissing, singing, quivering, alive. Paddy humming, Billy and Zekiel sweating up on the cordage round the big barrels on deck, wedging them in against the roll of the ship — against worse to come. My hand on the wheel began to learn the feel of her, to guess what she might do.

Then easier winds came, warm and thick and moist, and jumbled seas. *Rosie and Elen* sidled nervously along finding the wind.

Low black ragged clouds raced in from ahead, bringing bursts of rain and savage, blasting squalls. All hands, soaking wet, heaved at the sheets and halyards, clawed in canvas. The ship leaped, groaned, shuddered. Captain Paddy at the helm squinted through the rain, eyed the compass — hummed. The sea washed green around our knees.

Eldon said: "One hand for yourself and one for the ship, Tom. You're no use over the side." Wet, cold and tired — hands numbed, raw. Hard, hard going and I was frightened at the start, especially at night. But happy. Yes happy, in this tough little ship with her tough crew of real seamen.

Good friends. My loss was still there. A dull ache of longing for the way things used to be. But they filled the emptiness. I was not alone. I was one of them.

The wind settled at nor'west. The sky cleared. The sun shone. The sea sparkled. Gulls swooped and soared, scrubbed white like the puffs of cloud. Diamond spray flew over the windward rail. "Civil weather," Billy called it. He pointed ahead.

A streak of cloud, low down. A smudge on the horizon. *Rosie* lifted on the swell, racing westward; lifted again and now I saw it — a round-topped distant hill.

Land! The first I had seen since England. It was land.

We beat up towards it. I could see dark green forest crowding to a cliff's edge, and the cliff dropping sheer to the sea. A wild and empty shore.

My new land.

* * *

Eldon called up from the galley: "Tom, slip down for'ard, will you, with a bite o' the fish-and-brewis for yon passenger. He's well enough now!"

I'd forgotten all about him. The weather and the excitement and my new friends had pushed the whole terror of the shipwreck into the back of my mind. Now it flooded in on me. The heeling ship, the thunder of the surf, cries in the dark, the tearing waves, that feel of helpless fear, then the dreadful, hopeless loss. Behind it all lay that fog-wrapped nightmare game of hide-and-seek with Dirk Black — the wretched little sparrow quivering in his hand. The feel of death . . .

"Tom," Eldon again, "move along now. He's bedded down in the sail locker."

I pulled myself back from the past enough to

take the steaming fanny from him. *Rosie and Elen* was heeled well over to port and I climbed backwards down the canted fo'c's'le ladder, out of the crisp clear sunlight. It was dim below decks. It took a moment for my eyes to get used to the gloom.

The bunks on both sides were empty. A black square showed in the forward bulkhead — the open door to the sail locker.

"Hello," I called. "Dinner."

A grunt, half asleep, from forward. I barely heard it over the sound of the water around the bows.

I picked my way along, steadying myself on the bunk rails. The sharply canted deck, the bow lifting and dipping and the poor light made it quite a feat to keep the fanny from spilling. I made the forward bulkhead, braced myself at the sail locker and peered in. I couldn't see a thing.

I said: "Too dark to see yourself eat in there. I'll get you a light."

"I'm all right." The voice was thick and muffled.

"No trouble," I said. "Who are you? I'm Tom Penny."

No reply.

I wedged the fanny in the corner of the bunk, found the lamp and began to work up a light.

"You're the other lucky one off *South-down*, eh?" I called over my shoulder. Hope was still alive in me.

He replied something which I couldn't hear.

"You didn't see anyone — anyone else, in the water?" I asked. "My mother — and . . . "

"No." A low flat 'no.' "No one, lad. Only you and me."

I moved the lamp to the swinging bracket on the forward bulkhead and turned up the wick. It cast some light down into the black locker opening.

"There. That enough to see what you're eating?" I retrieved the fanny, and ducked my head inside the sail locker. "Here you are."

It was almost pitch black. The water noise sounded even louder in here and there was a musty smell of old canvas. A dark form was stretched out on the sails.

He grunted and moved a little, rolling over.

"Can you take the fanny?" I said. "I've got a spoon in my pocket." I passed it in. A hand brushed mine and took it from me — it was an odd feeling — I dug out the spoon and lifted the lamp down. I must see who this was.

I crouched again, with one hand on the locker doorjamb. The circle of light from the lamp spread slowly back across the sails.

"Tom, me lad!" The voice. Rasping. I knew it. I jerked back.

Too late. His hand clamped around my wrist. A huge hand with black tufts of hair on the back. The stump of the missing third finger bit into me like a claw.

There he was, now, his face framed in the blackness, catching the glow of the lamp.

Dirk Black!

His eyes were set deep under the heavy brows. There was a thick growth of beard on his chin and his lips were cracked and puffed. A grin spread across his face, though.

"Glad to see you, Tom. Glad to see you," he grated, "you're a sight for sore eyes, you are. Told me they'd fished a young 'un out besides me. What a piece of luck for the two of us. Never expected to see anyone off of the old Southdown, let alone you."

Friendly words. But my wrist was held like iron. And his eyes in the lamplight bored deep.

We stared at each other, our faces a foot apart. Fear stabbed at me as it had before. I must have shown it.

"Bear up, Tom. Bear up," he said. "Startled you, did I? I must have looked pretty much like a ghost to you, eh? Can't blame you for being took on. I weren't so surprised, though, I kind of thought young Tom Penny might get clear. Yes," he laughed, "always said, I did — 'That Tom Penny, he's a tough one. Don't say much — but he's smart.' And here you are — why, us two, we can travel together, we can. I'm minded to go up Onslow way when we get to Québec."

I found enough voice to breathe. "Let go. Please let me go."

"Now, now," his voice wheedled a little.

"You're not feared of Dirk Black? You're not thinking back on my little jokes — back in the old *Southdown* are you? That's just my way, boy. Frightened you half out of your skin, did I?"

He laughed and laughed, but his eyes watched me like two flints. His fingers bit into my wrist and he pulled me slowly, slowly towards the locker. Inch by inch. Closer, closer to that black hole, the laughing face. I tried to pull back but his strength was too great. Surely he wouldn't harm me here, crippled as he was.

My wits came together. The lamp! It was still there. In my other hand. I swung it high, yelled: "Look out!"

His eyes caught it, he dropped my wrist and I jumped clear.

I backed away, panting, my eyes held by his face framed there in the gloom. He was laughing, still laughing, and the sound of it filled the shadowed cabin.

"Tom, boy," he wheezed. "Tom, you're a mouse, you are! Never seen a shipmate o' mine take fright like that. You know me, don't you? A little game — just like always — it's my way. Tom. You just shorten sail and come alongside here again and we'll have a little talk —"

I was crouched at the bottom of the ladder, my eyes fixed on him, held there by his voice, his eyes.

" — a little talk about the wreck. Wreck of the old *Southdown*. Shame it was. All them good people — fish food. Not us though, Tom. You and me, we're inboard. But all those others — the whole lot . . . Ever seen a drowned man, Tom?"

Silence. I couldn't speak.

"Or a drowned . . . woman?"

His laugh burst out again and it went on and on.

He was evil, twisted. When it pleased him he would snuff me out, just as he had snuffed out that sparrow. He had said it himself, back on the *Southdown*. Back there in the fog.

I groped my way up the ladder, hearing his laughter still. Then I was in the sunshine, the wind blowing fresh on my face. I leaned against the hatch, quaking.

Spray slashed inboard, showered my back. I could only squat there, stunned, staring at the lamp I still held in one hand, at the deep red marks of his fingers on my wrist.

Black — why should Black have been spared? Why not Mother? Barnaby? But Black! He meant to do for me, I knew that.

Why? I didn't know why. I only knew he would do it one day — one day.

Now I had to live with his shadow looming behind me. Now I had to watch every minute. Until — I shuddered. Of a sudden it was cold.

7. The Battle of Grosse Île

The great river narrowed and shallowed. Trees pressed down to the shore, a solid wall of green.

One hand stayed forward watching for shoal water, lead line at hand to sound the depth. Two lay on deck ready to tend sheets and stays. Paddy or Billy took the wheel. The other stood down to tend the galley. On each ebb tide the river rolled seawards. We anchored and flopped down to sleep — one hand at look out — 'til it turned.

They helped Dirk Black up on deck for some fresh air and sunshine. He lay on a sail, his leg in its splint, and he kept up a running banter with the crew. I watched him and I kept well clear and I said nothing.

Further upriver there were rows of little whitewashed houses by the water with their narrow fields carved from the dark forest behind. Here and there the hills showed patches of gold and red among the green. Tricky channels meant anchoring at night, working upriver in daylight on favourable tides. The weather stayed cool and clear.

"Lower end of Île Orléans ahead, Tom."

Paddy squinted into the sun. "She's the big one. Québec's upriver aways still. Twenty, thirty mile." There were farms and fields in view on the island.

"Yonder's Grosse Île — off to port, see the high one there with the shoal running out?"

He called out: "Billy, me son, let's show some colours there!"

Billy hoisted the Union flag to the mainsail gaff. Then he ran up a strange red and white checkered flag at the starboard spreader.

"Little private signal that, Tom," said Paddy. "My friend — M'soor Untel — that's what he calls himself, though I doubt that's his name — he'll be watching the river and he'll send a boat out to tell us the 'rendezvoo,' as he says. We just drops in back of Grosse Île and waits for the word. No one lives on Grosse Île. Nice and deserted like."

He saw my puzzled look. "Ease sheets, Tom." I ran forward nudging Eldon awake as I went by, and checked away on the jib sheets. Elson tended the main and fore. *Rosie and Elen* paid off, headed for the down-river end of Grosse Île. I ran aft again.

"Ye see, Tom," Paddy said. "Trading's profitable, but mostly a man can make a deal more by — well, forgetting to pay the duty — specially on rum. Jamaica rum fetches a fine price in Québec. Usually M'soor Untel finds us a nice quiet spot to land it like. We got a few barrels along with the molasses."

Oh no! I suddenly felt empty. Paddy and the crew — smugglers! Lawbreakers! Pirates, footpads, smugglers — they were all the same. Cutthroats, surely. Men were hanged for smuggling. And I was helping them. Me!

Paddy, Billy, Eldon, Zekiel? Surely they couldn't be smugglers! But Paddy had just said that they were. Still, they had a reason. They couldn't live fishing. They'd been driven from home, driven to smuggling.

We rounded the shoal below Grosse Île.

"A couple o' bummers ahead, Captain," called Eldon.

Two open boats under sail came into view from behind the island. They bore down on us. Paddy eased *Rosie and Elen*'s bow up into the wind and we lost way. There were five men in the lead boat, four in the other. The leader sailed close up alongside and a man in the sternsheets cupped his hands and called up: "Ahoy there, Captain, Monsieur Untel wants you to discharge certain cargo at Grosse Île. I'll follow you in."

Paddy saluted happily, and put the wheel up. *Rosie and Elen* gathered way. We tacked up into a nicely sheltered little cove, dropped sail except for the main, headed up into the wind and anchored smartly fifty yards off shore. We lay there almost surrounded by the steep, wooded hills, with the mainsail shivering in what was left of the breeze.

What was I to do? I was actually smuggling.

We could be caught! We could be trapped in this little bay. But perhaps we were safe enough. They had done this many times before.

Paddy said quietly: "Turn the anchor cable up short. Keep everything on a split yarn. We just might want to make sail in a hurry like. Billy, a word —"

Billy and Paddy whispered together for a moment. I watched the two boats moving in. I felt tense and uneasy.

They came alongside — one to port, one to starboard — and dropped their sails. Their crews climbed aboard — nine men in all including the leader, a portly, swarthy man with a very dirty shirt and crumpled stock and a black tail coat. He had an enormous bulbous red nose. He spoke to Paddy, puffing somewhat.

"So, Captain, I am authorized to take the special cargo you have for Monsieur Untel to shore right here."

He handed Paddy a letter. He opened it and glanced at it — upside down in fact, because Paddy couldn't read.

"Aye," Paddy grunted. "Take your pick, my friend."

The visitor pointed to the barrels of rum lashed either side of the foremast.

"We've four like that. Break 'em out b'ys."

While Paddy and Black Jacket haggled over price, we cleared the lashings, set up a derrick and rigged a block and tackle to sway the big heavy barrels out over the bulwarks.

Our visitors weren't too handy and gave us little useful help, but the first barrel went down quickly and gently enough into the boat on the port side. Two of their men went down to settle it in position. Black Jacket leaned over Rosie and Elen's bulwarks giving hoarse orders to his men. He spoke English, and as they seemed to speak only French, they scarcely paid attention.

His coat was hitched well up over his broad rear, the tails askew. I caught sight of a fat document with a red ribbon on it sticking out of his hip pocket, and I took a couple of steps closer. I picked up a rope at his feet, reading what I could. It was folded, but I could make out one side of the heading, and that was quite enough.

At the top was the King's Coat of Arms — or half of it — then:

W A R R

Be it known

Jacob Cors

Deputy Customs

Is hereby author

APPREHEND any vessels and pers

Customs officers! We were caught! Caught absolutely red-handed. The trap was set. Smugglers — all of us — and me too!

Panic struck. Not me. No. Not me! I didn't know.

I didn't know! Tom, tell them I'm on their side. I'm only on board by chance. Tricked.

Tricked into helping. I'm a prisoner. Yes, that's it. I could even help capture the rogues! Quickly, tell Black Jacket — quick, Tom . . . Tom . . . !

Hold hard. Paddy is your friend.

The deck was crowded with sweating men, heaving at the barrels.

Decide. Decide . . .

* * *

Yes, a friend is a friend.

I sidled over to Paddy, whispered urgently: "Captain. He's a Customs man! He has a warrant in his pocket."

Suddenly, I was trembling. We were squarely and completely and hopelessly trapped. But I had chosen my side.

Paddy didn't look at me. Very quietly he said: "Thanks, me son. Now back to work."

Had he heard me? He didn't even look at me. He repeated: "Back to work, Tom — jump to it now!"

Baffled, I went back to help with the second barrel. Billy passed a hemp strop around it, doubled it through and dropped the eye over the hook on our hoist. We heaved away and the barrel eased off the deck. Billy swung it out over the side.

It tipped a little, slipped, then held. It slipped again. Billy fumbled, shouted: "L'kout below."

It paused a moment, then it plunged.

There was a screech of terror and a splintering crash from the boat below. We rushed to the side. The big barrel had snapped the mainsail yard, broken the thwarts and splintered the bottom. The boat was filling with water. The two crewmen jumped about wildly, uncertain whether to stay or abandon ship. Black Jacket shouted. One man tried to move the barrel and he let the water in faster. The other found a bailer and frantically scooped water out — a good deal slower than it came in.

Eldon and Billy shouted too — threw down ropes. Zekiel rushed for the long boat hook, swung it down and knocked one man over the side. He bellowed for help. Black Jacket shrieked at Paddy and jumped up and down, waving his arms.

Paddy soothed him: "What a terrible thing! And to happen in my ship. Just look at your boat! Now you just leave it to us. We'll put our dory down and bring in them two barrels what's in the water. You get into your own boat and we'll pass you down the other two." The barrels were already standing on their ends by the starboard bulwarks.

Black Jacket muttered darkly to his men on deck. Three of them piled over the starboard side into their remaining boat.

Paddy watched them go down. Then very quietly he said: "Stand by."

Our crew stood poised, alert, ready.

"Now!"

They moved like lightning.

Zekiel took two steps, felled a man with one tremendous blow, turned to the next, picked him up and hurled him over the side like a rag doll. Billy and Eldon had the next man over in a flash. Screams and splashing sounded from below.

Black Jacket was quicker. He stepped back and pulled a pistol from his belt as Paddy moved towards him. His thumb hooked around the cock, snapped it back. The pistol came up. Then —

I hurled myself at the back of his legs. The pistol roared in my ear. Powder burned my face. He came down on me like a sack of flour. Paddy was on him, then the rest.

"Over you go, then!" A shout, a shriek of rage and Black Jacket joined his crew in the water.

On the port side, two sodden figures were struggling aboard from their smashed boat. Paddy, Eldon and I charged, flopped them back in the water.

Back to starboard. The three in the water were frantically splashing about trying to get into their boat. Those in it were rooting under the foredeck, tugging at a sail. They dragged it clear. I could see the glint of steel.

Muskets!

There was a pile of them. Uncovered now, gleaming. The first man had one in his hands, pulling back the cock — I shouted.

Billy had an axe. With two mighty swings he knocked in the tops of the barrels standing by the bulwarks. Zekiel bent his knees, wrapped his huge arms around the first barrel. With one mighty heave he lifted it up and tipped it over the bulwarks. A torrent of thick, gooey, black liquid poured out into the boat below. The barrel followed with a crash and an echoing scream. Then the second barrel — I could smell molasses, not rum; molasses! Another great sticky, gluey, black glob poured down on the heads below — then another crash as that barrel landed in the boat.

It was a shambles. The boat was half filled with sticky, black molasses. The muskets were completely submerged. The men were floundering, cursing, shouting.

Billy cut both boats adrift with quick slashes of his knife.

"Come on, Tom. Hoist jib and foresail."

Eldon and Zekiel were already heaving in the anchor. Billy and I ran away with the working jib halyard.

Zekiel roared: "Anchors aweigh."

Paddy called: "Starboard tack, b'ys." I sheeted in the jib port side and joined the rest at the foresail peak halyard. Zekiel suddenly noticed the unconscious man lying in the scuppers. He pounced, picked him up like a baby, ran aft and dropped him in the water neatly beside the molasses-filled boat.

Paddy spun the wheel, our bow paid slowly off to port. A puff of wind caught the jib, the great mainsail began to draw and *Rosie and Elen* slowly picked up way. We hoisted and set the foresail, and trimmed the main. The water gurgled under our stem. We looked back on the scene of our dazzling victory.

It had all happened in a flash. There was one customs boat barely afloat, the other filled with molasses-covered crewmen slopping about in the black, sticky, clinging morass. They were shaking their fists, roaring, raging, cursing. Over it all came the quavering, cracking, helpless, desperate screeching of poor old Black Jacket.

Zekiel bowed deeply to Eldon and solemnly shook his hand. That did it!

We held our stomachs and laughed 'til it hurt. I could hardly breathe. Zekiel lay helpless, rolling over and over on deck. Billy and Eldon flopped across the taffrail completely out of control. Paddy's shoulders shook so hard he could barely steer. The ranting faded astern and at last I could draw a breath.

"Paddy — oh Paddy! I thought — I thought for sure you didn't understand —" I managed.

"Tom boy, I can smell a Customs man in half a gale! Besides he was English. All M'soor Untel's men is Canadians. Speak French, you know."

He grinned from ear to ear. "Trickery, that's what they was up to. We'd broke no law by bringing cargo upriver and just anchoring, so long as we didn't land none without paying the duty. Them fellers wanted to get just one barrel o' rum ashore, then they'd have us. Could have done it, too! They was right ready with all them muskets, eh?"

Billy giggled weakly: "They'll shoot naught but balls o' taffy now, I reckon!"

Prince William was happily licking at a gob of molasses dripping from the bulwarks.

"But Paddy," I said, "that was rum he bought. How is it —?"

"Wrong, Tom, wrong. He paid for rum because that's what it said on the barrels. Now you don't suppose old Paddy Isnor would sail from Nova Scotia clear to Québec with eighty barrels of molasses and only four of rum, do you now? Why, it just happens, Tom, that the markings on the barrels was already switched about when I got 'em off of the smuggler — er, the importer — down Nova Scotia. Molasses don't fetch much attention, it don't have no duty and it don't fetch much of a price, neither. Not compared to rum."

He chuckled happily. "So, Mister Customs Officer paid me cash for four barrels of rum and he got four barrels of molasses instead — he picked them out himself, mind." He laughed again. "He got no rum and he got no evidence — and he'll not get off Grosse Île in a hurry because he got no boats to his name.

"We can make Québec by midnight, lads. We got a flood tide. We'll be unloaded and away afore them fellers has that molasses combed out o' their hair!"

"Must be wasps aboard of Grosse Île, eh?"

Eldon chortled. "They'll have a right good meal!"

"Bears, maybe, too!" Billy collapsed again.

The breeze was back in the north. We rounded Grosse Île reaching fast under full sail. There ahead was a small lugger, three men aboard, all waving their hats. A red and white checkered flag snapped jauntily at the masthead.

Monsieur Untel!

* * *

After nightfall we slipped in alongside a stage in a dark little cove below Québec. I could see the lights of the town climbing the great cliffs in the distance. Above them, the sky was brilliant with stars. Monsieur Untel's men were waiting for us. They worked quickly and quietly, speaking only French. I couldn't understand, but our crew seemed to manage. In any event, the eighty barrels of good Jamaica rum were smoothly loaded into drays and hauled off into the night. Rosie and Elen lay alongside — lightened, fretting at her lines, somehow restless to get back to sea.

We went below and gathered round the table, tired, happy and light-headed with success. Billy poured steaming mugs of hot rum toddy all round. "A tot for you too, Tom. You're a real seaman now."

Paddy turned to Monsieur Untel.

"Lad here saved my life, you know. That devil had a pistol on me, and young Tom took his legs clean out from under him."

Monsieur Untel nodded with approval, his eyes twinkling. He raised his mug to me: "*À toi, mon vieux! À ta santé!* Your health and may your strong right arm continue to confound the enemy."

He lit a long cheroot. Paddy and his crew lit their pipes. The little cabin filled with smoke, the fumes of toddy and the talk and good cheer of old friends.

Monsieur Untel spoke very precise English with a distinct accent and a scattering of French words. He was a most elegant gentleman, dressed in the height of fashion. He wore a watered silk stock, brightly flowered waistcoat and cutaway jacket, knee breeches and brilliantly polished top boots. He had a long face with a big hawk's nose and very big black eyebrows. He smiled and laughed a great deal, and when he did he showed a flash of very white teeth against his dark face. On deck, when he had first come aboard, he had stretched a good foot taller than Paddy.

They told him of the rescue off Sable and of Dirk Black still crippled down below. The story of Black Jacket's defeat had to be told and retold over the rum, of course. By the time Paddy had finished for the third time, a Customs crew of twenty-four men, armed to the teeth, had been repelled and literally drowned in molasses!

Monsieur Untel wiped his streaming eyes with a spotless white handkerchief.

"*Messieurs*," he said, raising his mug, "here is a toast to the next time old friends meet — and to our new friend, Tom Penny." Mugs clanked together. We all drank.

"Tom here will have to get by Québec and on to Montréal quiet like," said Paddy. "If them Customs men was to spot him —"

"But of course," Monsieur Untel smiled. "Our comrade in arms. He can safely stay with me until I can arrange a safe passage."

"Done," said Paddy. "And Tom, you're due your share on the cargo."

I tried to refuse. He held up his hand: "Half a seaman's share for half the v'yage. Fair's fair, Tom. You earned every penny. The b'ys want you to have it and that's the end on it."

Monsieur Untel paid Paddy for the rum. Paddy handed me two sovereigns, a Spanish dollar, and three American dollars. I put it carefully on the table in front of me, almost afraid to touch it. I had never seen that much money before.

Paddy said: "Tuck it away in your belt, lad."

I shook my head. "No, Paddy. No! I helped you because you're my friends. But I can't take — can't take —"

"Can't take what, Tom?" It was Monsieur Untel. He looked at me very seriously, and the cabin grew silent.

"Well — I can't take —" I managed to breathe it out, "smuggling money."

"Tom," he said slowly. "That is for you to decide. You must tell yourself what is right and what is wrong. When a man is alone that is hard to do. Is that not so, *mon capitaine?*"

Paddy nodded, silent, his lips pursed. Then his face cracked into its old smile.

"Aye," he squeezed my shoulder. "Right enough, Tom. Here's my hand — and fair weather to you, b'y. Fair weather to you!"

I packed my few belongings in the bag Zekiel had stitched for me.

Monsieur Untel pulled out his watch. "Zut! It is late, Tom. *Allons-y. Au revoir, mon capitaine —* gentlemen." He rose, bending forward under the low deckhead and led the way up the ladder to the velvet night.

Billy's voice broke the silence from forward.

"Captain. Did you see that there Black? He's not below. Don't see him nowheres."

My heart missed a beat.

"Why no, Billy. No. We've not seen him."

"Must of jumped ship then. Left the fo'c's'le all of a clobber. Could be he took a ride on one of them drays?"

"A body'd think the sliveen might of give a nod to say thank'ee." Paddy spat over the side. "Well, he's no loss. That leg weren't so poorly, then."

Dirk Black. Ashore! Somewhere there ahead of me. In the dark. And able to get about. My scalp crawled. If he ever found me alone . . .

I almost panicked, almost changed my mind. I turned to Paddy. I nearly asked him if I could stay. But no. Dirk Black couldn't stand in my way. I had to go on.

I joined Monsieur Untel in the darkness under the trees where his horse was tethered.

"Tom," he spoke quietly, cinching up the saddle, "if those Customs men were to see you they would certainly recognize you. No doubt you would end up hanged or in prison. The prison here is so very unpleasant. And that Corson, he would have no scruples in using unpleasant ways to — ah — persuade a young fellow to tell what he knows of Monsieur Untel, *hein*?"

He looked down at me steadily, his cheroot-end glowing in the dark. "We must take no chances. No chances at all."

He mounted quickly, then gave me a lift up behind his saddle.

8. The Bourgeois

Smoke poured from *Aurora*'s side-by-side funnels. The paddle wheels churned. Mile by mile the banks of the great St. Lawrence River flew by. Whitewashed farms pressed side by side as we neared Montréal and the fields behind stretched golden in the afternoon sun. Fears of Black lay far behind.

Captain Tremblay was a jaunty, humourous little man — short and round as a barrel. He seemed always to be standing on the tips of his shiny pointed boots, trying to see further ahead. He kept up a running fire of talk to me in English between his orders in French to the helmsman and his shouts down into the yawning, hissing, rumbling engine room below.

Montréal had a busy harbour — sailing ships at anchor and alongside, steam vessels chuffing about their business, great rafts of timber floating down with the current, barges, small craft under sail, and my first sight of bark canoes paddled very swiftly by brown-faced Indians.

Down on the foredeck the wretched clutch of immigrants stirred among their baggage. Men, women, children, a sickly-looking lot. Lucky enough, though, to have lived through the ocean passage and the fever. They were together, too. Miserable and frightened perhaps, but together.

The paddle wheels slowed, steam hissed. We moved along more gently. Stone buildings lay along the waterfront. The familiar smells of tanneries and breweries and stables reached out. The river bank was steep here and ships lay crowded alongside, working cargo.

Captain Tremblay, up on his toes, spotted a space ahead. He reached for the steam whistle lanyard, tugged a series of jaunty toots and tucked *Aurora* neatly into the bank between two other steamers.

It was evening now. The sun slipped behind the mountain above the town. I stayed on the bridge watching the horde of passengers as they staggered off with their boxes and bundles. They were completely ignored by the sailors. Once ashore, though, they were beset by barrow boys and porters shoving for the right to haul their baggage and squabbling over the price.

"*Canaille*," sniffed Captain Tremblay. "Room enough for immigrants in Upper Canada. They want them. They can have them. So long as they do not stay here, though, with their thieving and their land-grabbing."

I thanked him for the passage, a little afraid that he included me with the rest. But he smiled. "A pleasure, M'sieur le Sou, any friend of Monsieur Untel, as you call him, deserves the best. Did I not tell you that my family have all come from his *seigneurie*? Since — oh, almost forever? Now, you told me you wish to see Jamie Mac-Pherson. Monsieur MacPherson is, of course, a Scotsman — well known — very noisy and very rough. Like many of them, he is, what one says — *nouveau riche*? He has spent many years in the fur trade. A bourgeois with his brigades of canoes and voyageurs. He stays now mainly in Montréal. *Un homme d'affaires* — a man of business. Very, very rich — a big man, that's for sure!

"To find Jamie MacPherson, Tom le Sou," he continued, "you should walk through the market place up there." He pointed to a tall column of stone topped by a statue. It rose high above the surrounding buildings. "That is a monument to the English Lord Nelson who defeated the ships of that *parvenu* Bonaparte, *n'est-ce pas*?

"Then you go left along Rue Notre Dame, and pass by the Cathédrale at the Place d'Armes. There you will see the Montréal Bank, and a little further along in Rue Saint-Jacques you will find Beaver Hall. As the Scots themselves will say, Tom, 'Ye canna miss it'! You will stand outside and listen, and if you hear the roaring of a bull, then Jamie MacPherson is in his bureau. *Comprends-tu*?" He grinned.

I nodded in confusion, shook hands, said good-bye and set off with my bag through the crowded, muddy streets. A strange town, this, all new and raw and fast a-building.

I found Beaver Hall quickly enough and I found Mr. Jamie MacPherson's rooms and his clerk, who was sitting at a high desk just inside the door. He looked at me with distaste. I was certainly a filthy, untidy sight. The last few days had left their mark on the remains of my clothing. I suppose I must have looked like a beggar.

The clerk was young, neatly dressed with smoothly combed hair, and a very high collar rising almost to his ears. He held a quill in one hand. He looked me carefully up and down, then with great precision he said: *"Va-t'en!"* He pointed his quill at the door.

I stood puzzled. He pursed his lips and said: "Go — away."

I found my voice, and quavered: "Please sir, tell Mr. MacPherson that Admiral Hardcastle said he might help me." I swallowed hard while he regarded me thoughtfully and wrinkled his forehead. Then he nodded, got down from his stool, walked across to a big, highly polished door and entered the next room. In a moment he was swept back out by a roar of laughter and followed by a huge bear of a man with a mop of shaggy red hair.

"Hah! Wha' have we here, Gérard?" His voice filled the room. "A friend o' the Admiral's, d'ye say?"

He looked around the room, spotted me half hiding by the clerk's desk and stopped, hands on hips, legs spread apart, looking down at me with an expression of cheerful surprise. He really was a giant of a man and he had a craggy, scarred, pock-marked face. His nose was bent to one side and quite out of shape, and a part of one ear was missing.

"So you're a friend o' Admiral Hardcastle's, eh, laddie? And what do you call yourself, now?"

I stammered: "Tom Penny, sir. I — I — come from Edgeham. In England. I — I —"

A huge arm circled my shoulder and he swept me into his room. It glowed with polished wood. There was a rich carpet, comfortable chairs, pictures.

"Sit ye down and tell it all to Jamie, laddie."

I started in a jumbled way to tell him that we had been the Admiral's tenants. And about the land and the shipwreck. And Mother. Suddenly I felt completely alone, and my voice died in my throat.

He spoke gently then. "It's a big, rough world, Tom Penny," he said, "but you're man enough. Aye." A pause then. "Have ye any other family but your uncle?"

I told him about Will. "Then I'll write to the Admiral to tell him of you — and your mother. Now, it's the end o' the day and you'll come along with me to take some dinner — you look hungry enough — and we'll surely see that you get on your way to Onslow. That's up the Grand River — a wee bit past the Chaudière. It's nae far. Did you ever paddle a canoe?"

I shook my head.

"You'll learn," he growled, "you'll learn."

He turned his head and roared: "Gérard!" The clerk appeared in an instant. "Gérard, we're off. Get word to Alec MacTavish tonight that he'll have a working passenger from La Chine with his brigade tomorrow. Name of Tom Penny — an Englishman, mind, and no bigger than a chipmunk — but something tells me he can paddle and carry with the best. I'll take him up with me in the morning."

Gérard nodded silently. Mr. MacPherson slapped his knees, stood up and rumbled: "Now, Tom, we're awa'." I followed him out into the busy street, running to keep up with his great strides.

His clothes were remarkable. A tailcoat and breeches — very elegant — but in place of a waistcoat he wore a many-coloured sash. The tasselled ends swung by his knees, nearly reaching the top of a pair of high, beaded moccasins.

We headed back towards the Place d'Armes. The street was narrow here and lined with tall stone buildings, some of them with shop fronts. Gentlemen were leaving their chambers, shutters were slamming closed and a lamplighter was working his way along the street. Carriages and dog-carts and wagons clattered by.

Mr. MacPherson seemed to know everyone and everyone certainly knew him. The younger gentlemen tipped their hats with a most respectful "Evening, sir." Mr. MacPherson wore no hat and greeted them all with a cheerful wave and their first names.

In the Place d'Armes we perched on the edge of a horse trough.

He said: "I like to do this every evening for a wee while, Tom, just take a stroll and sit somewhere watching the people go by. Yes sir," he went on. "People! Look at them, Tom. All kinds. Rich and poor, strong and weak, canny and stupid, lucky, unlucky, good, bad. French, Scots, English, Indian, Irish. Some have been here for generations and gone nowhere. Some arrived from nowhere and made a fortune overnight. It takes all kinds, Tom. See those laddies over there?"

Half a dozen short, stocky, swarthy men were crossing the square. They were dressed much alike in red woolen caps, coarse shirts, leather leggings and moccasins. Coloured sashes like the one Mr. MacPherson wore were tied around their waists. The ends swung as they walked. They puffed at their pipes, chattered and shoved each other about cheerfully — all a little the worse from drink.

"Voyageurs, *les mangeurs de lard* — 'pork eaters' — 'goers and comers'. They have lots o' names — some good, some bad ... " He chuckled. "They're the laddies who paddle the canoes and carry the trade goods to the *pays d'en haut*, and bring the beaver peltries back to Montréal.

Without the strong backs of a few thousand of those fellows, why the rich gentlemen of England and Europe and the States wouldn't have quality felt hats to wear. Now wouldn't that be dreadful?"

He laughed: "Dreadful, aye. Beaver hair's the best for making felt, o' course. That's why I never wear a hat. Can't stand the thought of wearing on my own head something that could be making me money if someone else bought it! Why, if I were to buy a hat, it would really be costing me double!"

He bellowed with laughter, and nearly elbowed me into the horse trough.

The voyageurs came abreast of us, stopped and greeted Mr. MacPherson cheerfully and most politely. The oldest of them — a squat, graying man with a big stomach and one wandering eye — chatted for a minute in French, grinning and nodding his head toward the others. Whatever the joke was, they all shouted with laughter, then teetered on their way.

"Aurèle Le Gros and his crew," said Jamie. "They're off wi' Alex MacTavish tomorrow. It's a special brigade, the last out of Montréal 'til next spring. Good time to travel, except the water's low. No mosquitoes. Good man, Aurèle. He'll drink his men under the tables of every tavern in Montréal tonight, and he'll have them all at La Chine and ready to go come morning — you'll see.

"Come to think on it," he said seriously, "if it

out of the warehouse carrying big square packages done up in canvas. Clerks checked off each one and a voyageur at each canoe directed the loading. Gathered by the far wall was a crowd of women and children — farm people and Indians, they looked.

Jamie's voice boomed out: "*Bonjour, les gars!*" The whole yard paused for a moment, grinned to a man, shouted a greeting, then turned back to work.

"Morning, Alec!"

Alec MacTavish appeared from the crowd. We dismounted and Jamie presented me as the working passenger bound for Onslow Township. "And no nonsense, Alec," he said. "Work it is. He's not to get his share of my food less he paddles and carries with the rest. I think, though, you might have him carry your smaller packs. The ninety-pounders could be a wee bit too much for a start!"

"Aye." Alec eyed me, scratching his chin. "Can't weigh much more than that himself. Still the rest of the men carry two, you know."

He seemed a dour sort. He was young, but he had heavy black side-whiskers and he was soberly dressed in a black suit — very formal — and a tall hat. He looked quite out of place among the milling voyageurs with their sashes and their bright shirts and caps and feathers.

"There's many an immigrant family trying to wheedle a ride up the river, Mr. MacPherson," he went on. He had to talk loudly over the yard clatter. "I've been turning them down for days. Steamers can't handle them all — even if they could pay the fare. They're a weedy lot. English, Irish mostly — half starved. They'd eat their own weight and carry naught. Immigrants — pah!"

"Dinna forget, Alec, people make trade. Times change and the man who changes with them makes the dollars. Now look'ee, Alec. I've money I want to put into steamers — like we talked about before. You keep a clear eye open this trip for channels and places for canals — and write me."

"Steamers — aye. Had a seafaring man here just last night, looking for work in steamers. A sail man, mind. Clean-cut, big strapping fellow, strong as an ox. Getting about on crutches, though. Seems he broke a leg at sea."

The noise seemed suddenly stilled.

A seaman with a broken leg? Dirk Black. But there must be hundreds of seamen who jumped their ships in Québec, looking for work. With broken legs, though? Black. Who else? I searched the crowded yard, moved close to Jamie.

He was eyeing the loading operation. "When will ye be set, Alec?"

"Half six now. We'll away at eight," Alec said. "I'm still missing a few *engagés*."

"Aurèle?"

"Aye. Aurèle and his boys."

"Dinna ye worry — they'll show."

They talked on but I took in nothing.

Dirk Black! It must be him. He must be following me. If he wasn't after me why come upriver at all? He was a sailor. He belonged on the ocean. Why not stay in Québec 'til his leg was mended, then sign on a sailing ship there? Because . . .

Jamie said: "Come inside, Alec, now. We've got business, Tom — you stay out here. Keep your eyes open and ye'll know a sight more about it all, time you leave." I hardly heard him. My eyes darted about the yard, looking for Black.

This would be the place to come. La Chine. Anyone going up the Grand River or the St. Lawrence — anyone going beyond Montréal had to go by La Chine.

If he spotted me here . . .

I sidled back to the wall, slipped under an idle wagon and crouched there in the shadows, straining for some tell-tale sound, watching the legs going by, waiting for a glimpse of a crutch, a swinging, bandaged leg.

* * *

Jamie came out of the warehouse, looking about. I swept a glance round the yard, then slipped out from the wagon and strolled over to him, eyes shifting, alert for some familiar shadow.

"You'll be on your way now, Tom." He smiled down at me, strong, reassuring. "You'll make a fine farm up there and one day you'll tell me about it. Promise?"

I nodded, uncertainly. When would I ever see him again?

I think he sensed my doubts. He waved his great paw of a hand up the river. "It's a huge land this, Tom. Even when a man's been clear across he can hardly understand how big it is. But there's not so very many people, and not so many of them that make things move, ye ken? And there's only one highway west. The Grand River. The likes of you and me, laddie, we'll be meeting again, you'll see."

He held out his hand. Mine disappeared completely into his. We shook hands and he pressed something into my palm. It was a coin — a gold sovereign.

"Now awa' wi' ye! Alec!" he bellowed, "it's nigh eight o'clock. What d'you think you're doing standing around? Move yourself, you don't get to where you're going 'less you make a start."

Alec came over, solemn-faced, carrying a short paddle. The great company of voyageurs filtered out from among the women and children, moved to the bank and settled into their canoes.

"All right, laddie," Alec said, "here's your paddle. We're awa'."

I followed him to the shore. Every canoe now had a flag flying from its stern. With the brightness of the voyageurs, their feathers, gay shirts and sashes, and their red paddle blades, they made a brave sight. Alec pointed to my place near the middle of the first canoe and I settled myself on one of the packages. He stepped aboard into a comfortable spot, just ahead of me, obviously made ready for "the bourgeois." No paddling for him!

The great canoes nudged out into the canal with short easy strokes, moving towards the open river. I looked back and there was Jamie, mounted again on his horse, his red hair blowing in the morning breeze, one arm held up over his head.

Alec lifted his hat. As one, every paddle raised on high. A mighty roar leaped up from two hundred voyageur throats. The paddles dropped, dug deep in the water. Voices called the beat in French. Twenty great canoes surged forward.

For an instant, behind Jamie, I could see the light of the open gateway leading out of the yard. Dark in its centre stood a lone figure. He had wide, hunched shoulders and one leg hung clear of the ground. Under each arm he held — I was sure of it — he held a crutch. I froze. Heads in the next canoe blocked my sight. I shrank, moved my paddle, tried to blend with the others, still craned around, looking. Not there now. The gate was closed to view.

A clear strong voice sounded right behind me, striking up the first of a song.

"*En roulant, ma boule roulant.*"

The whole brigade roared back:

"*En roulant, ma boule.*"

Then:

"Derrière chez nous y a-t-un étang."

And back again:

"En roulant, ma boule ... "

And off we set, flying up the broad St. Lawrence, bound for the Grand River of the Ottawas, shouting out the chorus of our song to the beat, beat, beat of the paddles.

La Chine, Montréal, Québec, the sea, lay behind. And Dirk Black with his crutches — I was leaving him behind, too — for a time.

I thought of his voice — "In my own good time, Tom, I'll snuff you out — just like — that." Yes, it must have been him back there in the shadows. Hunting me.

My paddle dipped harder. I was hunted by a madman. He had sworn to kill me. Why? It didn't matter why. When we stopped paddling for a pipe, I looked back. At the portages, I watched fearfully for other canoes behind. When we camped, I hardly dared set foot beyond the circle of the fire.

Whippoorwills at night, an owl, the loon at dawn, the start of rising ducks — they set my heart to beating. He was behind me. I had one way, one place to go. Sooner or later he would catch up with me. Sooner or later Dirk Black and I would meet again.

9. The Grand River of the Ottawas

Three days on to the Chaudière. Three days of paddling where the river spread wide and of carrying, poling and tracking at the rapids. Three days of blistered hands and aching shoulders, of sweating, singing and laughing — they were cheerful company, the voyageurs — of eating from an iron pot cooked over a wood fire night and morning, and sleeping on the ground under the overturned canoes. And all the time I watched behind me, fearful.

A few lonely farms were carved from the wooded shores, but we scarcely saw a soul on the way up, except at Carillon. Here, where the river crashed down over vast shelves of rock, was a sprawling camp of tents and cabins. Hundreds of men with their oxen, barrows, spades and picks were building giant earth dikes — for a canal, Alec said, with locks to lift the steamers by the great Long Sault.

Above, at Grenville, lay a steamer loading cargo. Her name, *The Union of Ottawa*, was painted across her paddle wheel casing.

"That's the first of them, Tom," Alec said, "first steamer on the Grand River. There's two or three now. Aye, and there'll be more. Jamie Mac-Pherson and his friends, they talk of canals up past the Chaudière and Chats Falls and Calumet and clear up the Mattawa to Lake Nippissing. On even to Lake Huron. No need of canoes this side of Fort William then, I suppose. Suits me. Trade'll move faster. Cost a packet, though. Still there's money to be made. Canals, shipbuilding, timber . . . "

We neared By's Town early next evening. The sun was low in the sky ahead, half-shrouded by a layer of thick, black cloud. Sombre, cedar-topped cliffs rose from the south side of the river. The twin falls of the Rideau plunged over, rolling out their curtains of spray. Across the river, the Gatineau flowed down from the north where the hills rose dark and distant. Vast rivers, rushing water and the forest. Little else. A wild and lonely land.

The brigade swept around a jutting cliff. In a bay to our left, the works of the Rideau Canal, a confusion of stone and mud, horses and working men. Across the river, a straggling settlement, and ahead of us, barring the river, lay the Chaudière Falls.

Water churned down between rocky islets. A boiling white cauldron swirled and tumbled, fed by water thundering down from around a huge rock horseshoe. Spray soared high and hung in the air, almost hiding the low blood-red orb of the sun. I could make out the lacework silhouettes of bridges crossing the channels — one even spanned the great cauldron itself. On one side, a random jumble of huge logs hung stranded at the horseshoe's lip.

We landed on a gently sloping shore below the Chaudière, close to the settlement and almost opposite the entrance to the new canal. Fires sprang up and cooking started — peas and fat pork, as usual. I was setting up Alec's tent — all but the bourgeois slept under the canoes — when he said: "Hold on, laddie, I think I'll have a little comfort tonight. There's an inn here, and I'll have my last decent meal and my last night in a proper bed 'til next summer. You could use a good scrubbing, too. We'll have you home in the morning. Besides — I think we're in for a little rain. The Columbia Hotel's the place for you and me. Come on."

We walked up the slope, away from the encampment and towards the village. It was a jumbled assortment of log and stone buildings — houses, a church, stores, warehouses and mills.

"All built by old Philemon Wright, Tom. Timber. That's where his money is. Enough trees back there in those hills to last forever. Lumbering. Aye. There's the trade for making money. And the Jonathans — the Yankees, ye ken — they're the shrewd ones at it. Old man Wright — he's one — and canny as they come."

We passed the King's Tavern, then further up the rise came to the Columbia — a big two-storey stone building with a verandah facing the river. The fires of our brigade encampment were below us and across the water we could still see the cliffs and the canal works, lights twinkling up here and there. The Chaudière rumbled away to our right, with the last of a blood-red sunset behind.

So this was to be our nearest town. It was an odd little clutch of buildings. The fields had tree stumps poking up through the ripened corn. The roads were no better than tracks. Everything had a half-made look — perched there on the river bank, as though one good flood would wash it all downstream together with the people who had ventured to build it.

Alex sucked gloomily at his pipe. "You know, Tom," he said, "if a man happened to be looking for trouble he couldn't find a better place. Nothing much else here but trouble. It's the last settlement going west, ye ken. There's no law and order. Besides settlers and lumbermen and rivermen, there's hundreds working on the canal. There's Scots, Irish, Canadians, English, Yankees, Protestants, Catholics — they all hate each other — can't think of anything else to do in their spare time but drink and fight. And there's a distillery right here sells whisky at two shillings the gallon. Aye — if Aurèle and his laddies are looking for trouble tonight they'll find it. Hope I don't lose too many men."

He paused a moment and said, almost to himself: "A distillery. H'm . . . that could be a good business, now."

We opened the door and stepped in under the sign announcing:

"Columbia Hotel — Bert Barton, Prop."

* * *

In the morning the stars were still glittering as we broke camp and carried over the Chaudière Portage, past the great cataract itself, then the Petit Chaudière rapid. Yellow streaked the sky behind us. Overhead it lightened, drowning out the stars. We poled up the Remic and paddled to the foot of the Rapide des Chênes. The birds cheered us across the portage with their morning songs. Then we were away, along the broad spread of Lac de la Chaudière.

The rising sun warmed our backs, the paddlers' songs rang out, the water was dappled with the early morning breeze and the sky above was a cloudless blue.

My paddle dipped with the rest and my voice joined the song. My long journey was nearly over.

At the first pipe of the day, I gnawed my lip impatiently. Here and there, on the left hand shore, I could see the beginnings of a farm — a distant cabin, a clearing, a thread of smoke. On the other side, to the north, the trees along the shore rolled up and up to a high, bare, rocky ridge.

An hour later, at the second pipe, my excitement began to rise. I could see where the lake narrowed ahead. In an hour I would be at my new home. Uncle Matthew would be there. In my mind, I could see the farm — green fields running to the water's edge, ripening corn, a snug cabin and a barn, chickens in the barnyard, perhaps a cow . . .

On we swept through the gap at the lake's end. The current pressed hard against us. Then the river opened wide.

Flung across our path was a mile-wide wall of rock and churning water. A wild white row of chutes crashed down between dark pine-studded islets and black, sharp-toothed rocks. A sombre, awesome sight. Its roar reached out to meet us.

Alec tapped my shoulder. "The Chats," he said (he called it "Shaw"), then pointed to the right. "Must be your place over there. Bert Barton said that Matt Penny was right up by the falls. That's Onslow Township on the north side, and I don't see any other cabin."

Just below the falls there was a bay. At the edge of the rocky bank the forest had been pushed back a little. A tiny, rough log cabin sat there, facing the river. A small canoe leaned against its side. The pines pressed hard behind it and their tops towered high and black against the sky. There was no sign of life.

"Here we are then, laddie, home and good

luck to you." The canoe edged in. Two men jumped waist-deep in the water, holding it clear of rocks.

"Stay a while, Alec." Suddenly I felt alone.

"Thanks, Tom, but I must get along. The portage goes over that island in the middle. We've a long day ahead." The men swung me out, grinning their good-byes. My bag followed.

I stood on the rocks and looked at the cabin. Its window stared at me like a single sightless eye. Pines and rocks and cedar. No green, growing fields, no Matthew there to meet me — just the rumble of the Chats and the forest's gloom.

I looked back at Alec. I suppose my slumped shoulders showed my feeling. He said a word to his guide and jumped to shore. The canoe moved off.

"Thanks, laddie," he said. "I will stay, just to make sure I turn the merchandise, ye might say, over to your uncle." He clapped me on the shoulder. "He must be around somewhere. His canoe's here. We'll find him. Then I'll scramble up along the rocks and my canoe'll pick me up above the Chats, when they've reloaded."

We climbed the rocky bank. I called: "Uncle Matthew!" The words echoed back. Only a blue jay answered. I dropped my bag at the empty cabin door. There, carved deep in a half-peeled log, was: "MATTHEW PENNY, JULY 14, 1829." This was home.

Behind the cabin, a rough path started into

the trees, and Alec led the way. Deeper in the darkness the water's rumbling faded. Faint and far ahead I could hear the *thunk — thunk — thunk* of an axe.

"That'll be your uncle, Tom." Alex smiled. "I'll awa'. Like Jamie MacPherson said, laddie, you and me — we'll meet again. You live right on the highway," he swung his arm up and down the river, "and I'll be by." We shook hands and said good-bye.

Out along the line of islets the brigade was crowding into the portage. The first of the great canoes was going over, upside down, on the shoulders of four voyageurs. Far across the river a thread of smoke rose in the still air — another settler — at least within sight! My eyes strayed downstream. No canoe, no movement, no Dirk Black.

I turned and ran deeper into the cool dimness of the pines, my feet flying over the silent carpet of needles, towards the axe.

The track took me through the stand of giant trees, then over rough-laid logs through a tangled cedar swamp. The ground took a long rise then through hardwood trees. I ran on and on, jumping rocks and fallen logs, and the ringing of the axe grew loud and near.

Suddenly I was on the level in a narrow clearing. It was about two hundred feet long, dotted with stumps and roughly heaped with slash. The morning sun caught the green and gold of the topmost leaves and the sky shone blue above.

On the other side, stripped to the waist, shoulders rippling, his axe swinging a steady solid beat, was Uncle Matthew. I stood there, breathing hard, watching, listening to the solid sound. I was there. At long last I was there.

I watched for a long moment, rooted to the spot. Then he stopped. He sunk his axe into the trunk of the tree, turned, pushed back his hat and wiped his forehead. He picked up a wooden bucket and raised it to his mouth. Then his eyes caught me over the bucket's rim. He stopped, frozen for a second.

"Tom!" he shouted. The bucket dropped and he bounded towards me. "Tom Penny!" I started across the clearing and in a moment I was wrapped in his great bear-hug, swung off my feet, whirled around, danced amongst the stumps, flung high in the air, perched on his shoulders and jigged around the clearing. He dropped me to my feet and we stood there looking at each other, laughing like a pair of fools.

10. The Cabin at the Chats

"Well then, Tom, it's you and me. Just you and me."
We sat outside the cabin in the last of the evening
sun. Matthew sucked his pipe. I gazed off, past the
wildness of the Chats, at the distant trees across
the river.

I had told him of the shipwreck and Mother,
of Dirk Black and Paddy and his crew, of Jamie
MacPherson and Alec, and the shadow of Dirk
Black behind me. It all came out with hardly a
stop for breath. When I finished I felt drained
and empty, and my eyes filled with tears. Matthew put his arm firmly around my shoulders
for a moment, then without a word strolled to
the shore to check his fishing nets. It was
almost too much for me. All those dreadful
happenings of the last few months and now this
awesome forest; our "farm" a jumble of rock
and giant trees and gloomy marsh, our home a
tiny cabin.

Matthew had built it with the help of Rory
O'Donnell from across the river. The walls were
cedar logs, notched to fit roughly together. The
cracks were stuffed with moss and clay. It had a

single-pitched scoop roof of hollowed basswood and a wooden chimney.

I groped my way inside. It was dark and I stumbled in the gloom. There was no flooring other than some flat stones at the door and by the fire. A little light came in the window. The Quartermaster Sergeant at By's Town had issued Matthew a dozen panes of glass and some putty, along with an axe, a saw, nails, blankets, a kettle, some tools and some powder and shot for his old musket. Little enough altogether. But at least it shut out the forest. Room for Will, too, when he came.

The cabin darkened as Uncle Matthew came quietly through the door. He stirred the fire, added logs. A handful of pine cones gave a cheerful blaze. He lowered the trammel so the big black iron pot hanging on it was close over the flames. Then he carried a flaming spill to the wick of the tallow lamp, and closed the door.

"It's not much, Tom," he paused, "yet. It's been lonely. I'm glad you're here. Now it's home. Your father and mother — they'd have made a fine place here — in time. For you and Will."

Another pause. I nodded. His words were very quiet. Not like him.

"Look," he said suddenly. "What's done is done. Your father and me, we soldiered together. Waterloo and all. A lot of our friends died. You have to understand, Tom, when your number's up, it's up. And that's it." He poked the fire again and stirred the pot. "I can't be mother and father to you, Tom. I don't know how. But I can be your partner. How's that? Let's the two of us be partners. We share everything. Decide things together. We'll start right now. I'm not your uncle any more. I'm Matthew — right?"

His hand was out, and he was looking at me very steadily. My eyes were dry now, and I put my hand in his and I whispered: "Partners — Matthew — partners."

We stood in the clearing in the chill gray of the early dawn. "Another acre for this fall, Tom. Two of us now, we can finish it off, cut it and burn it — have it ready for planting before it freezes." Matthew pointed with his axe handle. "Those beeches and oaks, though — we'll have to burn 'em up here for the potash, with all the rest. Not like those pines on the knoll down below."

I said nothing. The clearing seemed so small. The trees towered above us. The forest was endless and still. And here we were, the two of us — with an axe, setting out to carve ourselves a farm.

Matthew spoke quietly. He seemed to read my thoughts. "Big, isn't it? Only one way to cut the forest down, though, and that's one tree at a time, Tom. Let's get on with it."

So we worked all that day and every daylight hour for the next two months without a break. We cleared our acre and a little more and burned the brush. The trees were all hardwoods up there, tough to cut and heavy to move. The biggest ones had to be left standing and we girdled their trunks and all the trees along the south side of the clearing with deep-cut notches so they would bear no leaves in spring and let the sun get at our crop.

I learned how to use the axe. I sawed the smaller logs for firewood — hour by hour, day by day. I built a sled to haul them down the muddy path. The wood pile at the cabin grew and grew.

Matthew spent a few precious measures of powder teaching me to shoot his musket. Along with the clearing work, I took on the task of keeping us fed.

Geese swept across the sky in huge clamouring vees — thousands upon thousands of them, heading south. Our bay filled with them each evening and I could shoot at least one if I crept down to the shore before dawn with the musket and waited for the light.

Rain and wind stripped the leaves from the trees. The birds showed clearly now; bluejays flashed and shouted through the bare woods, woodpeckers and chickadees dipped and darted. The summer birds, robins and swallows, the kingfishers, herons, thrushes and sparrows thinned out and slipped quietly south. Deer were easy to see and I shot what we needed. The place was alive with raccoons, *"chats sauvages"* the Canadians called them. Matthew said that was how "the Chats" got its name. They were clever thieves and none of our food was safe unless it was hung high from a branch or securely latched in the cabin. For a time pigeons swarmed in such flocks I could knock them from the trees with a stick. A fishing line from the canoe below the falls would always hook a good-sized pike.

Little by little, I began to love our corner of this great, wild land. There was so much here — so many new things to see if you cared to look, so many new sounds to hear. I found myself shouting back at the bluejays, cawing at the last of the crows, hooting at the loons.

The forest was a little less awesome now. Each tree that Matthew's axe brought thundering down added another little victory. Bit by bit our cleared land grew and every inch of it was ours.

We sat at supper one late fall night. It was cold outside and the fire blazed warm and bright. We ate and we talked about the work to be done by winter.

Matthew said: "We've got the time still to cut some of those big red pines on the knoll. Eight of them there, must be over a hundred and fifty feet tall. Big job, but we can handle them, eh? Worth £50 apiece. Times eight — £400. Imagine that?"

He spoke between mouthfuls of a big goose leg. I had tucked the bird at the back of the fire to roast early in the afternoon, and when we came in at dark the cabin was hazy-blue with smoke and filled with a glorious smell. And the bird was delicious. Firm and fat with crinkled brown skin and enough rich meat for two meals.

"Rory O'Donnell, over Fitzroy way, said I could use his oxen. We can ask him if he'll come over, help us with the pine logs and harrow the ground up in the clearing too, before it freezes."

He finished the leg and wiped his beard and moustache. He kept them trimmed and very neat. Matthew somehow always managed to look crisp and tidy even after a long day's work.

"Delicious, Tom. That goose would do credit to the finest kitchen in England. And I had friends," he winked, "in every inn along the Portsmouth Road. Could always count on a first-rate dinner back in the kitchen while they were changing my horses."

He carefully cut a long slice from the bird's breast and put it on his plate. "Ah, but this goose," he sniffed it deeply, then slowly savoured a mouthful, "this goose was no barnyard goose — this was a free-flying, beautiful wild goose. And it was there for the taking — a pennyworth of powder, eh? That's all. And done to a turn, Tom. A meal fit for a king — a couple of kings. That's what we are, Tom, a couple of kings, you and me."

He pointed his knife around the cabin. "Look at us! Look what we have." The firelight caught his eyes. He smiled and his teeth flashed white and even.

"A roof over our heads. Warmth. Food a-plenty. Land. And up there those great red pines,

Tom. It's all for the taking. You know around here they only cut the big trees in winter. Easy to move them on the snow when the ground's frozen. Then they raft them downriver in spring. Those big fellows of ours, though, on that knoll — there's a good slope down to the water, and — well, I think it's worth a try. Good money for them. Good money."

He tugged his moustache into neat points, smiling at the thought. "And if we just leave them there," he went on, "anyone could come along this winter and —"

"Couldn't we sell them to someone where they stand?" I ventured.

"Might do, Tom. I could ask Rory O'Donnell. He's a lumberman. Works at it every winter. But if we do it ourselves, we get all the profit. We'll just cut 'em down, drag 'em to the river with O'Donnell's oxen and raft 'em to the Chaudière ourselves. Then young Oliver — he's Mr. Wright's clerk — very serious, he is — he'll say," Matthew puffed out his cheeks, " 'And now Mr. Penny, how would you like all the money for these fine sticks o' timber — Spanish dollars, golden guineas, American eagles, perhaps?' And I'll say 'Well, Oliver, my man, I'll take a few pistareens in small change, and I'll take ten pounds credit for supplies, and you may send the balance' " — Matthew tipped up his chin and snapped his fingers —" 'send the balance to our bankers in Montréal.' "

I laughed with him.

We had to take down several smaller white pines first so that Matthew could drop the huge reds where he wanted. It was a slow business axeing through the six-foot trunks, and when the first of them thundered down — just where Matthew planned — we cheered ourselves hoarse.

He wasn't as lucky with them all. Three of the giants skewed off into a tangle of bush. Five out of eight, though, I said to Matthew, that wasn't bad for a beginner. He chased me all the way to the cabin.

Rory O'Donnell lived across the river with his family in a solid, square-log house with a barn and some well-turned fields. He was a bouncing cheerful India-rubber ball of a man. He had a comical, round shining face with wide-open grey-green eyes and a mop of curly sandy-coloured hair that fell down over his forehead. When he talked, which was nearly all the time, his whole face lit up. His mouth split wide, his big nose twitched and his eyebrows danced. Even his ears wiggled. With his solid round belly he looked very much like a barrel on stumpy bowlegs.

I brought him across from Fitzroy in the canoe and he looked over our logs, hat tipped back, scratching his head, his hair down over his eyes. "Boys oh boys, we got some big sticks there! Looked at them pines meself, I have. Nearly took 'em too, but there's not much else around to make it worth a special camp in winter. May not get 'em all out now with no snow to skid 'em. And them white pines ye cut, Matt. They ain't squared up. Don't get too much for 'em like that. Still . . . "

It took us two trips to raft four oxen, a harrow, a stoneboat and a stack of hay across the river, and then we worked together solidly for a week. Rory and Albert, his hired man, cheerfully slept on our earth floor. His daughter Jennie paddled over each morning with a basket of food. She stayed to handle a yoke of oxen, then she put our evening meal on the fire and paddled back before dark, her boots and skirts caked with mud. I managed the second yoke, though not as well as Jennie, I must admit.

She was a little younger than I and cheerful enough. She really seemed a gay and happy sort, but her temper would suddenly flare — at her oxen, or over a pie squashed in the basket or when she slipped on the rain-soaked slope. She had two coppery braids and they bristled and twirled when she was angry. But when she smiled it was wide like Rory and her freckles ran one into the other and her grey eyes sparkled. She laughed as hard when I got tangled or fell as she cursed when it happened to her. We kept a sort of armed truce between us.

When all our logs were finally afloat in the bay we improved the log road through the swamp and took the animals up to our clearing. We pulled the smaller stumps, hauled off rocks and dragged away the logs we had not been able to manage ourselves. A good harrowing between the remaining stumps readied the soil and we sowed the first of our winter wheat. We were done before the snow.

After supper that night, the four of us sat round the table in the firelight over mugs of tea, well satisfied with our work. Matthew brought out the jug of whisky — for the first time since I'd been here — and the men had a good-sized measure. Rory O'Donnell sniffed it, his big knob of a nose twitching. Then he tasted it with great show, smacking his lips and nodding his head.

"Ah yes, Matt, and that'll be the best from Squire Wright's distillery, I'd say. A far cry from that wretched poteen they'll sell ye in Corkstown. That's by the canal cut at By's Town, Tom — ye keep clear of it."

Matthew nodded. "I brought this up in July. They do say it improves with age."

"That's so, that's so, Matt. But only to a certain point. I'd be thinking once the cork's out of it, ye know, it could spile."

Matthew grinned and poured them another tot.

"Matthew," Rory tipped back his stool, pulling at his pipe. His round cheeks shone in the firelight. "Now the job is done, I'll tell yez. After young Tom come over to ask for oxen and says ye're a-cutting them pines, I says to Peg, 'Oho, another Englishman, green as Irish grass, thinks he can lay a big pine down where he wants. Thinks he can just roll it down to the water any time o' year just like that.'" He snapped his fingers. "Ain't that so, Albert? All alike, they are — Englishmen. But ye done it, Matt. Ye done it. And we only had to leave two of them lie."

Rory tugged at his ear. He watched Matthew from under his mop of hair for a long moment, then he sat forward.

"Look'ee here, Matt, ye're a man knows how to work and how to do figures too, eh? Would ye mind to work for me this winter? I've run me own shanty — a lumber camp, ye know — up the Gatineau these last two years. Not many as goes up there and I've a contract to cut for Squire Wright. I used to work in one o' Wright's shanties up the Bonnecherre River. Learned the trade, 'fore I went on me own. There's good money in lumbering, Matt, and the Gatineau's wide open — every man for himself, it is."

He paused for a pull at his whisky, put the mug carefully back on the table. "Look," he said suddenly, "I found a wonderful big stand o' pine last winter. It's all ready to cut. I've all me men signed on, but I still need a shanty-clerk to keep the stores and the accounts and tally the timber. Twenty dollars a month and all found. Would ye like the job?"

Work for the winter! There would be nothing

for him to do here once winter came, other than improve the cabin and hunt and cut firewood.

Matthew's face broke into a grin. He slapped both his hands on the table and opened his mouth to speak. Then he stopped. "Thank you, Rory," he said, and turned towards me, "but I'll have to ask my partner."

It would be lonely here. My first winter and on my own. Then the thought of Dirk Black surged up suddenly from the back of my mind and I caught my breath. I swallowed hard and forced a smile.

"I — I'll be all right, Matthew," I said. "I'll see to things here. You go."

"Well, I don't know now," Matthew frowned.

"Come ahead then, the two o' yez. I need a chore-boy too to help the cook and all. Young Tom can have the job. Eight dollars a month."

Matthew looked at me. "Well partner, I'd say our cabin can look after itself." I nodded quickly.

"Done then," Rory broke in. "I'll meet ye at Wright's Village on Friday. I'm going to take Peggy and the youngsters down in the canoe for the fall fair. Ye float your raft down and I'll help ye with it at the Chaudière."

I nodded to Matthew. He smiled at me and together we said: "Right!"

11. Down to the Chaudière

Our monster pines lay in the water, lashed across with half a dozen smaller logs into a good-sized raft. We had a bark shelter to keep us dry for the passage, flat stones by it for a cooking fire and enough food and firewood aboard to keep us going for a couple of days. Matthew had made three long sweeps for rowing and steering and I had cut a few poles so that we could rig our blankets as sails if the wind blew fair. Our canoe went aboard as did pretty well everything we owned. Then Matthew thought that we might need an anchor so we rolled a hefty boulder up onto the logs and tied a length of rope around it.

Our raft was no thing of beauty and she was certainly nothing like the size of the huge ones I had seen further down the river, but she should get us to the Chaudière and she should certainly be worth a packet.

We christened her *Queen of the Chats*.

Back at the cabin for a final look around, Matthew took his knife and carved beside the door, underneath his own name:

M AND T PENNY, NOV. 14, 1829
BACK IN SPRING

We left the door on the latch, walked down to the *Queen of the Chats*, shoved off and poled away from shore. Then working the sweeps, we rowed slowly out of our bay towards the middle of the river below the falls. The current caught us and we crept smoothly out onto the broad calm waters of Lac de la Chaudière. All we had to do now was to keep out in the middle with our sweeps and the steady current would do the rest.

This was the day! The laziest, the most luxurious day — the day with nothing, absolutely nothing, to do. It was still and quiet with a white-grey sky. The hills climbed back from the river, grey with leafless trees. To the north the long bare-rocked ridge rose sharply, dotted with pines along its top. Off southwards, smoke rose in columns from countless clearing-fires, then spread out to hang in one long, low streaky layer. The only sounds came from low-flying ducks and the distant calling loons.

I baited three hooks with chunks of fat from our quarter of venison, and set up lines on poles wedged between the logs. Out here I should catch a pike, a big channel catfish or even a giant sturgeon.

Matthew gave one contented sigh then slept, flat on his back, mouth open, snoring. I settled down on my stomach to watch my fishing lines. They dropped straight down through the glassy water, the bait a dim white blob below. Shoals of minnows darted just beneath the surface.

I drifted like the raft, half-asleep, half-hoping I wouldn't get a bite. The loon's cry came long-drawn, lonely, saying good-bye. I woke late in the afternoon, shivering. It was chilly now. The clouds were darker and a fitful wind ruffled the river. Matthew shook himself awake.

"Could be some rain, Tom, maybe a storm. Should get over to the north shore." He yawned, stretched and pulled himself up. "Don't fancy stumbling down the Rapide des Chênes at night."

The sweeps were awkward and heavy. It was tedious work pushing the boom ahead of you, then lowering it to lift the blade from the water, then walking backwards along the logs for another stroke. The raft scarcely seemed to move.

However, within two hours we were alongside the bank and tied securely to the trees for the night. Our fire burned cheerfully enough on the rock hearth and we feasted on a beautiful big doré which had taken one of my hooks as we rowed.

A few drops of rain began to fall. I banked up the fire and we crawled into our blankets under the shelter and lay on our backs, talking lazily. Light flickered under our roof and the rain pattered gently. After a bit, Matthew's voice changed a little.

"Tom," he said. He paused as though he were

thinking out what to say. "I haven't told you this, but before you came young Robert Shirreff — from Fitzroy, you know — he came to see me, wanted to buy our land. Those Shirreffs are great ones for building canals. They see them all the way up the Ottawa and on to Lake Huron. And they have the money, they say."

He propped up on one elbow, reached out to the fire for a spill and lit his pipe. Then he settled back in his blanket.

"Robert said they fancied to cut through our swamp and the pond — said it would be the easiest way past the Chats. Seems to me it could be the only way."

He looked right at me. "Said they'd pay me a lot of money for the two lots. I told him I couldn't decide right then, not 'til Martha arrived. So he asked me to let him know whenever I had a mind to sell. Do you know what he said he'd pay me, Tom?"

I shook my head.

"A thousand pounds."

One thousand pounds. A fortune. I could hardly take it in. With one thousand pounds — he must be joking.

The rain was falling harder. It drummed steadily overhead. The fire hissed and crackled.

"What do you think, Tom?" His eyes were level; he meant every word. "It's a lot of money."

I felt suddenly cold. We couldn't sell the land. This was the only place — I tried to pick my words. I said: "Yes, yes — it is a great deal, but it's — it's our home, Matthew. It's the place we — we all picked out. Father, and — and we have the cabin there and we've started —"

"But Tom," Matthew rolled over and lay on his stomach, propping his chin on his hands. The firelight caught one side of his face. The other lay in darkness. "It's far more than the land is worth for farming. Besides, it's rocky and parts of it are sour, you know that. And there's the swamp. Settlers, when they come out here, they don't all get good land, Tom. They just get a place on a map. Some's good, some's not. No way to tell in advance. If you get a poor lot does it make sense to be stuck forever?"

I tried delaying, putting it off. I said: "Why don't we wait 'til spring — see how things go?"

"Don't you see, Tom?" he urged. "Mr. Shirreff has made an offer now, but it won't stand forever. He might find some other way around the Chats. We'd never get a thousand for it then. Might never be able to sell it."

He leaned nearer. "You just think of all that work over the last two months, Tom. And what have we got to show for it? An acre or two of ground planted, that's all. But look at us now! Only a couple of week's work and we're floating down on our own timber and it's worth real money — real money." He slapped his hand on a log and sat up.

"Remember that first big tree coming down,

Tom? Remember what a sight that was? There's thousands like that up those rivers. Thousands. All for the man who wants to go after them."

His eyes were bright now. "I don't mind hard work, but on something like the lumber business now, where there's real money. The cash from Mr. Shirreff would give us a start. We wouldn't have to just work for wages for Rory. Why —"

I sat bolt upright. "No, Matthew. No — no — no. It's our land — mine too. And Will's. We came to farm it. Father wanted to — he helped pick it out — and Mother wanted a farm. It's ours, Matthew. We can't leave it —" Panic grew inside me. Matthew wanted money. The land meant nothing to him. To me, it was everything. I couldn't leave it.

We stared at each other in a long tight silence.

"All right, Tom," he said evenly, lying back. I'm sorry I raised it. We'll have to wait and see how things go." He rolled himself in his blanket, his back to me.

The rain grew heavier, pounded against the shelter, hissed into the fire.

The flames died and I dozed fitfully through the dankness of the night.

At dawn it was cold and raining hard. Matthew and I spoke little. I got a fire going with some wood that I had kept dry under the shelter and we had breakfast and cast off. The raft moved gently downstream.

We each remembered roughly, from our upstream journeys, what we should expect ahead.
The first problem would be the Rapide des
Chênes. It was rough and about half a mile long.
Then we would have five or six miles of quite fast
water — including the Remic Rapid — wide and
shallow, but not too rough, just a question of
avoiding rocks. Finally, we would have to run the
Petit Chaudière, another half-mile of steep, wild
water ending in a wide, fast-moving pond that
tumbled directly over the Chaudière Falls. As to
the height of water at this time of year and how
to get the raft past the Chaudière, we had no idea.
Matthew decided to go on ahead in the canoe to
find Rory O'Donnell and look things over.

"You're in charge now, Tom," he said. "You
should have two or three hours drifting yet
before the first rapid. Keep yourself close to the
north shore and when you see the fast water
ahead, poke into shore or anchor her and wait for
me to come back — right?"

I nodded. We had been wary of each other
since last night's flare-up and I was almost glad
he was going. He paddled off and I was left on my
own.

The bare oaks along the north bank were just
visible. I could see nothing off to the south but
the greyness of the river and the rain. An occasional pull at one sweep or the other was
enough to keep the raft on her stately course. The
rain drove down endlessly and the shelter began

to leak. My jacket soaked through, my boots filled and when I went out to work the sweeps, water trickled down my back.

The morning dragged miserably by. I crouched in the shelter. If I stayed in one position I would warm up a bit, but as soon as I moved I felt clammy and cold. The rain eased up but a mist clung to the surface and it grew more and more difficult to make out the shore. Perhaps I should anchor. It would be hard to see the rapids ahead. How long had I been drifting since Matthew left?

I must have dozed off, sodden and chilled as I was. I woke — how much later? — cramped and numb, and had to force myself to move out of the shelter. I looked out to the left — you could hardly call it to "port" in this vessel — and could see nothing but grey. The other side was the same. Well, I must get back in sight of the north shore. I heaved away at the starboard sweep to turn the raft towards shore, then worked first the port then the starboard sweep to move her ahead.

No sign of land. I kept on with my "rowing," running from side to side between the sweeps. I was worried now. I could still see nothing but fog. Suddenly, I realized that I had no idea where I was, and I certainly had no idea of the direction I was pointing. The raft could have turned itself to any heading at all while I was dozing in the shelter. My frantic rowing could be taking me out across the lake, or back against the current, or — or even closer to the Rapide des Chênes!

Was I moving faster now? Yes, it seemed so — but how could I possibly tell? I could see the greyness of the mist and the rain-pocked water, and nothing else. There was simply no point in rowing blindly. Even if I knew where I was going, my single-handed rowing would make little difference. There was only one certainty. The current was going downstream and it was taking the Queen of the Chats and me straight to the rapid.

I must anchor. Now. The big boulder lay on the logs at the "stern" where Matthew and I had left it. The rope was still around it, tied to a log. I tried to move it. It was very heavy and it hardly budged. I got my fingers under it, braced my back and my legs and heaved. It made a half turn and then it wedged firmly in between the logs. The raft lashing must have stretched. The logs had separated a little and they held fast to the anchor.

Was that the sound of water? Running water?

I needed a lever. There! One of the sailing poles. I jammed its point under the stone, tried to lever it up, failed. There was nothing for my lever to work on. Some of the firewood — that's it! Place a log up close to the stone, so — now get the point of the pole under the stone. Pull down, down, down, now press — it's lifting, turning, rolling.

Ugh! The pole slipped out.

I fell flat, scrambled back to my feet. Yes! I had turned the stone over — it was halfway to the end of the raft. Once more now, and quickly, quickly.

That *is* water running.

Now! Move up the firewood. Make a fulcrum. Pole under the stone, press down, down again. Yes. Another turn. A foot to go now — once more will do it.

A quick look all round. Nothing but fog. The sound? Perhaps.

Again. This time the stone rose up to its point, teetered on the very end of the raft. I pressed down, sank to my knees, flattened the pole with all my weight — almost — almost.

I glanced up — the mist blew clear and I was looking out at a sweep of glassy smooth water and beyond it the riffle, the break, the top of the rapid!

I threw myself down on the pole with all my weight and strength. The stone shifted, teetered again and rolled.

Right over! It splashed! A big, deep, beautiful splash. I lay flat, breathing hard. The rope snaked out behind the stone — out — out — out to the end. It jerked once. The raft shook. The rope lay still. Still and slack. I leaped for it, pulled it in, hand over hand.

No stone. No anchor. No! Oh no! The rope! It was broken. The water was too deep. The stone hadn't found bottom. It had snapped the rope. In my panic I had dropped it too soon. I should have taken a sounding — any sailor would have checked the depth. Now I had no anchor — no way to hold the raft.

The fireplace stones! They might do — if I was quick enough.

I could hear the growl of the rapid now. It was getting louder. I dashed forward, picked up a stone, started back. I glanced to one side, and there was the rapid — very close.

The rumble had grown to a roar. Too late for anchoring now. I'd have to ride it out. The *Queen* was slipping along fast, moving broadside to the current.

I had to get her turned! To go down sideways could mean hanging up on a rock, breaking apart, overturning.

I grasped the port side sweep and backed hard on it, then again, and again. The raft turned slowly, slowly. Another couple of heaves would have her lined up. What then? I couldn't steer with the side sweeps in the white water. I needed one at the rear. I leaped for the spare sweep lying by the shelter. Frantically, I dragged it back and tied it to the centre log with the broken anchor line. I dug the blade into the water, heaved sideways — the raft turned — a little. I heaved again. It pointed for the rapid.

I could steer!

The water was shallowing now, smooth and

icy clear. I could see the bottom. It was slipping by beneath me, faster, faster. Big boulders below the surface now. More ahead. The water suddenly shallowed, then seemed to drop away from under the raft's bow. There was a scraping bump and the stern started to swing. I tugged at the sweep, tugged, tugged again. Water piled up behind me, boiled over the raft, pushed, pushed, ground it forward over the ledge. The bow was hanging now, out over the rushing water. Then it started to dip. The stern lifted and the raft shot forward over the ledge and on down the long churning, boiling white slope of the Rapide des Chênes.

Water surged between the logs, snatched at my legs. I clung to the sweep, swinging it with all my strength whenever I could hold my footing, trying to keep the raft pointed. It twisted, plunged and heaved downwards through the great, half-sunken boulders. A grinding, jarring, thump. We struck a rock, hung up, swung sideways, tipped, tipped over — over. I held fast to the sweep. The raft slewed, lurched, ground off, swept on again. The great logs leaped and plunged and tugged at their lashings. It was no longer a raft. It was a bundle of gigantic sticks, barely holding together. They churned and crashed and ground against each other. I balanced on one huge butt like a circus rider, holding fast to the sweep.

I could work the sweep no longer. I could only

try desperately to keep myself from being swept away, from being crushed by the logs. It was a nightmare of boiling water — plunging logs, roaring, shattering noise.

And then it stopped, just as suddenly as it had begun. We bobbed out below the rapid, the *Queen* and I, and we were still together. I stared stupidly at the place where the shelter had been. It was gone — swept away with everything we owned. The rocks had gone too. I had no anchor — nothing.

Slowly my numbed mind understood that I still could survive. The logs hung together. The three sweeps were still tied in place. I could float and I could steer.

The water was a little deeper here but moving fast. The bottom slipped by quickly below me. There was a long, shallow stretch and the Remic Rapid ahead — I remembered that — then the Petit Chaudière. It could be as wild as the Rapide des Chênes and it was about as long. With good luck I might get down. But the Chaudière itself — that was a different matter! No one could live through that.

It was still misty. I tried to guess the distance to shore, judge the time it would take to swim. Could I make it? Could I keep my direction? Should I try now? Or below the rapid and before the Chaudière? I peeled off my sodden jacket, picked at my boot laces, got them off, then tied them together and hung the boots around my neck.

And where was Matthew? Surely he should have got down and back by now. He must be looking for me.

I did have some time, though. It would take — how long — half an hour? — to reach the Petit Chaudière. The mist was clearing. I might drift closer to shore, or to an island. I waited, shivering with cold, trying to guess the time.

It was clearer — there was something off to the right. And away to the left now, I could make out the shore. But surely I could be seen. Matthew must be there, somewhere. There was an island coming up ahead and on the right. That would be closer. I might be able to swim to it. I stood poised, taking hold of my courage. But now the water was shallower and faster. Ugly rocks broke the surface.

Too late. I had left it too late. I would have to ride it out. The raft grounded with a jerk, threw me flat. Water surged over me, lifted the raft's stern, moved it ahead. It paused, teetered, then shot forward and plunged down through the roaring water. I swung the sweep, tried to keep straight. The raft swerved and bucked, jarred on a huge rock and spun like a top.

The sweep caught bottom. Its end whirled like a whiplash, caught me a monster blow across the chest and I flicked backwards off the logs.

I remember tumbling crazily, churning water, gigantic noise, helplessness, fear of death.

It went on and on and on. Flash of a boulder. A glimpse of tree and sky. A gulp of air. A crushing blow thrusting me down again.

Then it was quiet and dark and I hung lazily, idly wondering when the bursting ache in my lungs would make me breathe and suck them full of water.

The current must have rolled me over, swirled me upwards. It was suddenly light and I thrashed for the surface.

Air! I sucked my chest full, again and again. Vaguely, I took in that the water here was smooth. Behind there was white tumult. There was the raft — too far away. Trees on shore, moving. No, I was moving. Fast.

I remember tumbling crazily, churning water, gigantic noise . . .

A giant hand was pulling me. There was a deep rumble now. The low, growing growl of the Chaudière — I could feel it. Now I could see the spray hanging high, grey buildings, a jam of logs.

My mind said: "Swim. Try. Try to swim." I tried. I kept thrashing, kicking desperately. The clutch of the water, the falls edge near, the flash of boulders on the bottom, the massive roar. Then a sudden dark form above. The shape of logs against the sky. I was slammed amongst them. Water sluiced through, pinning me in. Like a matchstick. I was caught like a matchstick in the jumbled jam of logs on the very lip of the Chaudière.

I clung, helpless, breath sobbing in my throat, willing my strength to come back. At last I worked one arm firmly over a log. Inch by inch I pulled myself upwards. My legs in the water were suddenly clutched, torn to one side as I hung from the log overhead.

There was a shift then, a shuddering, heaving shift in the whole jam. It levered my log upwards a little and I was clear of the water clinging like a leech, but with strength to do no more.

The Chaudière roared, battered at me. My mind could only say: "Hold fast!"

Another shift, and my log took a sharper angle. I clawed myself upwards a few inches and held there again. How long? I hardly knew.

A tangle of roots lay over my head like bars against the sky. There was no way up. The water raced beneath me. My log trembled faintly, lurched again, then again. I held. There was nothing else I could do. Any minute the whole shifting mass might twist, crush me, carry me with it over the falls. And that would be the end. I held fast and almost wished for it to come.

Something took my shoulder. Something clutched me, pulled me back from the log, held my arms, tugged. I tried to shake it off, but it held me, pulled me. I couldn't fight any more. Then across my chest I felt what it was. It was an arm.

And the sound in my ear above the roar of the water was a voice, shouting. There was a face close to mine.

Then I was lying on my back on the logs looking up at clear sky. Leaning over me were three figures and one was Rory O'Donnell. He mouthed something I couldn't hear and he grinned.

They half carried me across the jumbled logs. There, between the jam and the rocky shore was a gap of about thirty feet. Partly bridging the gap was a huge log crib, tipped up at a crazy angle with water surging over it. Ropes led across from shore.

Men clustered on the bank. Arms waved. Someone behind me tied a rope under my arms. It tightened and jerked me ahead and I half scrambled, half scraped over the crib towards shore. I hung on the crib's edge a second, then I was flipped right into the rushing gap, and spun wildly for a dreadful moment. I thumped against the rock and was dragged up its solid roughness like a played-out fish on the end of a line.

I lay there, gasping and choking, heaving up water. My fingers clutched at the rock. I was safe. Stunned, battered, cold to the bone, shaking wildly — but safe, on solid rock, alive and safe.

People pressed in, shouting and cheering. And there was Matthew. He picked me up in his arms, carried me through the crowd. He swung me up onto the back of a wagon. I sat with my back against the side stakes, wrapped in a blanket, blinking at the milling people, still half drowned.

"Welcome back, Tom Penny. Welcome back," a shouting voice. "Strange way to come, I must say." It was Bert Barton. Round, laughing Bert Barton of the Columbia Hotel, standing at the front of the wagon, the reins in his hand. It seemed like years since Alec MacTavish and I had stayed at his hotel. He beamed down at me, danced a happy jig and his chins shook and his belly bounced.

"Up you get, too, Matthew. Up you get. Teaching this young fellow how to run the Chaudière on his own, eh? Quite a show. Had half the township here watching by the time Rory and his boys got that crib down. Nearly went over, too. Should o'seen it!"

Over Matthew's shoulder he shouted into the crowd: "Rory! Hey! Rory O'Donnell — Basile — bring your boys along. Come on. Climb up!"

My rescuers piled into the cart. Rory stood me up and we shook hands again and again in a tumult of noise.

Bert Barton raised his arms high above his head. There was a little less noise. "Boys, we're all to the Columbia to celebrate the rescue. And the first drink is on the house!"

A great cheer went up — hats flew in the air. The crowd swarmed around. Bert shook the reins and we paraded off, along the rough track. We were on the island which anchored one side of the horseshoe cauldron. We crossed the bridge spanning the waterfall and trundled along the rutted streets of Wright's Village. The crowd grew as we went — men carried children on their shoulders, boys dashed beside us and hung onto the sides of the wagon. Windows opened as we went by. It was like a circus arriving and Bert Barton waved his hat and cracked his whip as though he were the ringmaster himself. By the time we reached the Columbia Hotel it seemed the whole village was there. People swarmed around us and we were swept inside. Voices, cheers, laughter, congratulations, came in happy confusion.

"Hey, did you see the boy in the water? Smartest thing ever. Why —"

"I seen that raft go over the falls there. Reckoned if anyone was aboard they was goners. Why —"

"Rory, me bucko! Sure and yez were quick gettin' that crib down there."

"And who'll be payin' for it, Rory? 'Twas Ruggles Wright's, ye know —"

Laughter.

"An' the boy — powerful lucky someone seen him go."

"Basile Trudel — he was out there. Can't swim a stroke —"

"What's the use to swim? You fall in — you drown — an' that's for sure."

Bert Barton roared: "Boys. Boys. Give 'em room. Give 'em room."

He led us through to the kitchen. With my wet clothes stripped off, with towels and blankets and the hot stove, my shivering gradually eased. Matthew sat beside me, spooning hot soup through my chattering teeth.

Bert rushed in again, smacked a bottle of whisky on the table. "Fill your boots, boys. Why, that's the best crowd we've had here since they opened the bridge. This'll get them all in the spirit for the fair, eh Rory?"

"Spirits it is, Bert, and we'll drink yer health." He picked up the bottle. "Now, I daresay none o' yez'll scorn a drink o' Bert Barton's whisky, boys?"

It suddenly came to me that I had started all this by falling asleep on the raft. I burst out: "Matthew. It's all my fault. I fell asleep up there — I drifted away from shore. I — I tried to anchor but . . . we've lost everything. Matthew — everything . . . "

Rory O'Donnell broke in: "Not everything, Tom. Ye'll have your logs all right. I had some o' me boys ready below the Chaudière to gather them up. Ye see, we come down from Fitzroy for the fair, like I said. Matthew, he came in this morning and I told him how to take the raft down the rapids easy like. So he went back upriver to join ye on the raft and I was standing out on the bridge with Basile waiting for to see it come down."

He took a long pull at his whisky.

"Ye see, laddo, what ye're supposed to do is to keep to the north side and gentle your raft into shore at Rafting Bay. That's just below Petit Chaudière. Ye puts all yer clobber ashore there and ye sets yer canoe onto the raft andyou poles her out into the current. Then ye're supposed to jump in yer canoe and paddle ashore, all neat and tidy, and yer raft goes over the falls at the deep part. Sure, ye did fine, Tom, except ye forgot to stop at Rafting Bay!"

There was a bellow of laughter around the table.

Matthew squeezed my shoulder. "It's all right now, lad. It's all right. Couldn't be helped. And you're alive."

Basile Trudel raised his glass. "Here's to Tom Penny, the first man to try La Grande Chaudière straight! If those logs hadn't got in his way, he'd have made it for sure!"

Laughter again.

"Now boys." Rory O'Donnell pushed back his chair and stood, glass in hand. "We've had some fun today. Wasn't that a sight to see, Basile? Young Tom a-bobbing up like a cork and swimming right over to the eddy there, cool as can be. Only place in the river a body'd be carried into the log jam."

He turned to me and wagged a finger. "But once is enough, Tom. Once is enough. I'll have to say now, me buckos," Rory rambled on, waving his glass, cheery face round and red in the heat of the kitchen, his lock of hair hanging over his eye, "I'll have to be saying now — that's the kind o' luck belongs to the Irish. Must have some real old Irish blood in 'em, eh?"

A cheer. Glasses banged on the table.

"So Matt and Tom, they're going to work in O'Donnell's shanty this winter."

There was an icy hush, then a low growl. Faces turned to Matthew and me. Rory's eyes flickered around the table, and he plunged on.

"Och! You'll be sayin, 'But it's Protestant they are!' Well now, which would yez sooner have, eh boys? A couple of Englishmen as sticks together — good men in the bush — men as couldn't really help to be Protestants at all at all, seein' as where they was born. Or would yez choose," he glowered around at each upturned face in turn, "would yez choose — ye Patrick, Leo — would yez choose a creepin', crawlin', cheatin', treacherous, groggy-goin', rotten," he spat out the word, "Orangeman!"

There was a moment's pause. Big raw-boned Patrick at the end of the table brought down his fist with a crash.

"The Pennys. That's who I'd choose."

"Right ye are, Patrick. Matt's to be shanty clerk and it's Tom for chore-boy — and here's a drink o'whisky on it."

A roar of welcome went round the table. Down went the whisky. And Rory's boys — O'Donnell's shanty crew — took us in as their own.

12. By's Town

I woke with the sun in my eyes and lay there dumbly, wondering where I was, why I ached, why my hands were blistered and raw.

Matthew was hanging my clothes over a chair, stooping under the sloping roof. We were in a room under the eaves in the Columbia.

"Well, partner," he sounded cheerful, "you left the party early. Didn't even say goodnight! D'you know it's past eight o'clock? Can't lie in bed all morning."

He sat on the bed, his eyes serious. "That was a rough day, Tom. You're lucky to be alive. Let's just be thankful for that and don't you be blaming yourself for what happened. Look, we're both green as grass and we'll make a lot more mistakes before we know what it's all about, so don't worry your head about it.

"I've been to see Squire Wright's clerk and he's paid me £25 for all the timber that Rory's boys salvaged from the raft." He looked a little sheepish.

"That £50 a stick I was talking about is what they fetch delivered at Québec. You see, Wright's

144

men will have to keep them for the winter, then send them down with their own rafts in spring. Besides, two of the big sticks got damaged. Of course, I paid Rory for his men's work and for his oxen — he wouldn't take anything for himself. Said that was just being neighbourly. Basile wouldn't take a penny, either.

"I bought an axe for each of us and a musket to replace old Brown Bess, and — here Tom," he fished in his jacket. "Here's a knife for you. Basile says there'll be peddlars and Indians with goods to sell at the market over in By's Town this morning. You can get a sheath for it and we can get the clothes we'll need for winter.

"Why," he grinned and roughed up my hair, "if we mind our pennies we'll have a little left to spend at the fair this afternoon. Do you know, Tom, this is the first-ever fair at By's Town — it's a bright, sunny day and the whole world's going to be there!"

I groaned. I was warm and comfortable where I was.

"So up you get!" One quick flip and Matthew had me out of bed and onto the floor in a tangle of blankets.

We had a fine breakfast of bacon and eggs. It was a bright morning as Matthew said, but cold. A fire crackled in the hearth. Bert Barton would accept nothing for our bed and board. He winked and said it was the best night they'd had at the hotel for years and we had been the main attraction. "Imagine it! Next year we could bill you in advance. You know: 'See Daring Tom Penny ride the Chaudière Falls on a log!' Why, they'd come all the way from Montréal to see it!" Bert was quite carried away with the idea. "We'd fill the hotel up. We'd make thousands. I could take bets too. 'Ten to one, gentlemen. Ten to one on the Chaudière Falls!'

"Stay here 'til you go upriver with Rory, Matt. When will it be, d'you know?"

"Monday morning, I think. Depends on getting all our provisions and stores from Squire Wright's tomorrow. D'you think they'll open for us on Sunday?"

"No old Yankee that I ever knowed would turn down business just because it's Sunday," Bert snorted, his chins bobbling. "After church meeting, that is, and the meeting's always bright and early. Squire reckons the good Lord don't mind getting up same time he does, specially seein' as he built the church! Oh, by the by, Matt, you should call in at the Colonel's offices over at the canal works. Sergeant there — Jack Snell, his name is — told me t'other day there was mail there for you from England, in case I should see you."

Mail from England!

We almost ran down the track and across the bridges. The Chaudière tumbled white and sparkling in the morning sun. I could feel its spray. There was a crisp, cold breeze and a dark blue sky. A beautiful day and you could see your breath. We passed the mill on the last rocky island, then Isaac Firth's Tavern and a scatter of cabins in the cedars at Richmond's Landing. The road swung left here and climbed sharply, then levelled out at the cliff top.

It was muddy and rutted and stumps showed here and there, but it was cut wide and straight and it had a name — "Wellington Street" — proudly shown on posts at the corners. There were a few wooden houses — some of them quite large — standing among the stumps, and further on, in the high area on our left between Wellington Street and the cliff edge, there were three large buildings — barracks and the hospital, apparently. Flags snapped crisply above them and beyond to the north you could see the line of the Gatineau Hills, sharp-etched against the sky.

A little further along, the way dipped downwards to the canal diggings. Off in one direction stretched a great untidy ditch. Men worked ankle-deep down in the mud. Shouts echoed along the cut. Teams of oxen hauled at stoneboats and horses heaved at drays.

The other way, eight huge, half-finished stone-paved locks led down to the river like a giant's flight of steps. Here too there was a rumble and bustle of activity. Before long, ships would climb up from the river level, step by step, a full eighty feet to the canal cut above.

A big grey stone building was set close to

the locks, down near the river, and we were directed inside to the desk of the Chief Engineer's clerk.

He was not a military man. He was thin and pale with nervous fingers, a long face and an Adam's apple that bobbed when he spoke.

After a moment's thought, he said: "Ah yes. Mr. Matthew Penny. I do indeed have a letter for you." My breath caught with excitement. "It came with the dispatch box from Whitehall. Hmm — where is it now?" He sorted deliberately through a stack of mail. "Yes, here we are. I've been holding it for you. Do sit down if you wish, Mr. Penny." He spoke to Matthew with surprising respect. Getting a letter from Whitehall must have marked him as a man of influence.

Matthew turned the letter over, then deliberately cracked the seal and opened it. I watched his face as he ran his eye down the page, and I saw his jaw tighten. I could hear the clerk's pen scratching and the outside sounds and Matthew's breathing. He shook his head gently and he handed me the open letter.

It was from the Manor, Edgeham, dated 1 October, and it was signed "Henry Hardcastle." It read:

My dear Penny:
I do not know if the news has reached you, but I am informed that the brigantine "Southdown," which was carrying Martha and Tom Penny to Québec, foundered in

early August. She may have grounded on Sable Island as wreckage has been recovered by the people at the rescue station there, but they have had no sign or word of any human life being spared.

Unless God has been particularly merciful, I fear you must reconcile yourself to a tragic loss. I have broken the sad news to young Will Penny. Losing his father, mother and brother — all violently — in such a short space of time has been a very grave shock to him. The Vicar is keeping in close touch and I expect he should write to you soon.

Mr. Leech assures me that due to your foresight the William Penny holding legally falls directly to you. However I enclose a sworn copy of the underwriter's declaration of loss and a list of the passengers and crew, which could assist you, should there be any complications in completing the sad business of transferring the land title to yourself. Perhaps you may wish to assign a portion of it to Will.

I am sending this letter through the Duke's offices in Whitehall and I am sure it will reach you with utmost dispatch. I should mention that he has high personal regard for Lt. Colonel By, Commanding the Royal Engineers on the Rideau Canal. I believe he knew him in the Peninsula

during the Spanish war. I am sure Colonel
By would be pleased to forward letters for
you, rather than have you suffer the delay
of the regular post. You may show him this
letter — no doubt he will remember my
name. In any case, I will write to him. You
may find it helpful to be known to him.

Please let me know if I can assist you
in any other way . . .

The enclosed papers included a list headed:
"Lost at Sea — All the Officers and Seamen and
All the Passengers of the Vessel, Southdown.
Foundered on or about the tenth day of August,
1829."

I ran my eye down the page and the familiar
names leaped from it. "Arnold Bardwell —
Master. Charles Soulby — Boatswain. Dirk
Black — Boatswain's Mate. Martha Penny —
Storekeeper. Thomas Penny — Boy. Barnaby
Spar — Cook."

We sat there and my thoughts were forlorn
and far away. It was cold in the high stone room
and I shuddered.

Matthew squeezed my shoulder. "Come on
then, lad, we've things to do." He thanked the
clerk and I followed him dully out into the sunshine.

"Matthew Penny?" Just outside the door, a
heavy-set soldier faced us.

Matthew nodded slowly.

"I'm Sergeant Snell — Jack Snell. I'd like a

word with you, if I may. Just a short word — and private."

His eyes flickered at me. They were greenish, pink around the edges, and he had sandy-coloured hair and a mottled face. Something about the set of his shoulders seemed familiar, but there was no recognition in his eyes.

Matthew was curt: "Tom here is just as private as me. You can say what you have to say in front of us both."

"Come on, then," said Snell, and we followed him a little way from the canal, clear of the muddy road and the clatter of the wagons.

"Look here, Mr. Penny," he said. "I know your name because I've been doing some hunting about — on my own account, that is, nothing to do with the army, mind. I understand you own a double lot of land up at the Chats."

Matthew nodded.

"Well, I know a certain party — from Montréal. He is — ah, interested in buying some land up that way. Wants to build some sort of mill, I think — needs water power. He asked me if I could help him out — see if I could find something for him, you know. He has plenty o' money. Pay a good price. He wants the waterfront at the falls, o'course."

Our land again! I watched him carefully. His tunic was well-worn, but the stripes on his sleeve were bright and new, and his boots were clean — he didn't work in the canal. The smile on his face seemed a little forced, I thought.

He went on: "You see, Mr. Penny — I'm the clerk in the office here and — you know how it is, you being an old soldier yourself, like — I get to know who's who and what's what — and of course, a man has to look out for hisself. So sometimes I gets a little commission work on the side. Now if you'd like to name a price I can get in touch with my —"

Matthew interrupted him, coldly. "You desk soldiers make me sick, you know. Always conniving and twisting. Someone wants to buy my land —"

Snell wheedled: "Now, now, Mr. Penny." He spread his hands. "No offence. Business is business. I'm just trying to do a bit of good to the both of us."

"All right." Matthew was angry. "But first, I'll say this. I've given a person I trust first chance to buy the land for £1,000. If you, or your so-called friend, want to make me an offer, then out with it and let's see the colour of your money. I'm up the Gatineau on Monday for the winter, so if you want to talk about it and stay warm at the same time, you'd best be quick. You can find me at the Columbia."

He spun on his heel and strode off up the slope leaving Snell with a half-smile frozen on his face.

Our land. The Shirreffs. And Twiss, Cornelius Twiss — back in Edgeham. He had wanted our land for someone. Now it was someone from Montréal.

... The list from the Southdown. Mother lost. All hands, it said. But I was alive. So was Dirk Black ...

Snell was still gaping up the hill. I shook myself and broke off in a run. I caught up with Matthew where the bridge crossed the canal.

13. Away Up the Gatineau

Before dawn on Monday we started work down at the summer landing, loading Rory's four canoes. "*Canots du nord*," Basile called them. They were smaller than the Montréal canoes, but we managed to stow a tremendous load in each. Barrels of salt pork and flour, a chest of tea, sacks of peas, pots, kettles, axes, saws, grindstones, cant-hooks, tools, bedding, winter clothes — all of this went in plus five men to each canoe. There was very little freeboard to spare. I helped Matthew with his lists of stores. Basile directed the loading and Rory kept a sharp eye on the whole operation.

"Tobacco, Matt? Should have a keg of it somewheres. And pipes — a couple o' dozen. Oh! I did tell ye, didn't I, that I'll have no whisky in the shanty — excepting in the medicine chest. Ye'll mind that some o' the boys might think to smuggle in a little drop o' morning dew, to doctor themselves up on their own, in case of being took ill, ye might say. But I has my rules — so keep yer eyes open."

A chattering throng of wives and children gathered in the cold to see us off. Mrs. O'Donnell was there with Jennie and young Sean and the baby, and Basile's fat wife came down with her cluster of younger children. It was a grand mix of Irish, French and Indian, and very hard to tell where one left off and the other started.

Basile's oldest son, Fernand, was down for a last-minute talk with Rory, Matthew and Mr. Wright's clerk about the supplies to be brought up after Christmas. The river and the portage paths would be frozen hard enough by then to take the *traineaux* — the ox-drawn sleighs — and Fernand was to lead them up. In the interval, we would manage with the canoe cargo.

Someone whispered "Squire Wright," and the happy turmoil stopped.

A tall spare old hawk of a man came striding down the slope. He was straight as a ramrod, with a shock of white hair flowing to his collar. His eyes glowed under bushes of eyebrows and darted about taking in every last detail. He came straight over to Rory and shook him by the hand and his gaunt old face broke into the warmest of smiles.

"Morning, Mr. O'Donnell. You have everything you need, I trust. I instructed Oliver here to give you credit against delivery of your logs to me in the spring." He had a brisk, clipped Yankee way of talking. "I'll have my eye up for damaged logs, though. There's some mighty sharp falls and rapids on the Gatineau."

Rory nodded. "Fair warning, Squire. Fair warning."

"You should build chutes, you know. Like we're starting to build at the Chaudière. Get your logs round those rough parts. You'll lose a lot of them, otherwise. How far up are you going to be cutting?"

"Well now, Squire, that's a good question." Rory's eyes twinkled. "Not even me own men knows the answer to that. Fact is, I hardly know meself. Seems there's going to be another gang or two cuttin' up the Gatineau this year. I did hear that old Ironbound Burke has a contract too. Now would ye know where Ironbound might be cuttin'?"

Squire Wright laughed: "He wouldn't tell me either, Rory. But if I did know, I could hardly tell you, now could I?" His face turned serious. "I just hope you keep the peace up there. Fighting slows down the cutting, you know, and I want every stick you can get. Reckon you and Burke would be smart to join forces, work your boys together on the drive and sort out your logs when you get them down here. You'd save a lot of money, you know."

"Ah!" Rory spat, "I'm a reasonable man, Mr. Wright. But that Burke and his troop o' bog-born Orangemen! There's no workin' wi' them, ye know. Why, Burke won't even stick to one side o' the river. Last year was the first time anyone but me and me boys cut the upper Gatineau and now them hooligans is after shovin' me out."

Rory's eyes were snapping, and he waggled his finger up under Squire Wright's nose. "And if ye happen to see Mister Burke, Squire Wright, ye can tell him from me that any of his sneaky tricks like changing o' the bark-mark on me logs, or weaseling that rotgut whisky into the shanty and trying to bribe me boys, and I'll wrap a cant-hook right round his rotten neck, I will. And it won't be just fightin' with shillelaghs — it'll be muskets — and I'm ready for anything!"

He was hopping mad now, dancing from one foot to the other, and the Irishmen in the gang clustered behind him egging him on.

Squire Wright took it all very calmly. "Steady now, Rory. Steady. You're all the same, you Irish. Not happy unless you're fighting each other, are you?"

Rory calmed down a little and Mr. Wright went on. "I was born a Yankee, Rory, but I've got no wish to fight Lexington and Yorktown over again with the English. Neither do they want to fight with me. How would we do business? Why don't you Irish forget the Battle of the Boyne and Cromwell and all that ancient nonsense. Just because you're Catholic and Burke and his lot are Protestants . . . This is where we all live now, and there's problems enough right here." He shook his head. "Well, I guess I can't stop you fighting, but remember — I only pay for good logs safely delivered. The fastest way to ruin yourselves is to have a shanty war up there."

"Well sir," Rory said lamely, "if Burke keeps out o' my hair, I'll keep out o' his. Oh, Squire, this here's Matthew Penny, my new storekeeper, and his nephew, Tom."

The old gentleman shook hands very civilly. "Ah yes. You caused quite a stir at the Chaudière, I'm told. Sorry I missed it. Look, Penny, Rory O'Donnell must have some regard for you to hire an Englishman — and a Protestant, too?" Matthew nodded. "Perhaps you can talk some sense into these Irishmen — you'll have all winter to do it! Well, good luck to the lot of you." He shook his head wryly at Rory and stalked off, with Oliver the clerk half running to keep up.

There was a final round of embraces and good-byes and tossing children in the air, and we were off in the clear, early morning cold. Basile started the song:

"En roulant, ma boule roulant,"
Back we shouted:
"En roulant, ma boule,
Rory's boys is off to the bush,
En roulant, ma boule . . . "

Paddles dipped in time and we sped a mile down the Ottawa then turned due north up the Gatineau. The first five mile stretch was wide and pleasant with the sun just catching the tops of the banks. They were cleared and there was a fine-looking farm below the first rapid.

Above it the river narrowed and it was hard

going. In fact, it was the start of four solid days of endless back-breaking labour. The water was faster, the falls were higher and the rapids swifter, the loads heavier and more awkward, the portage paths steeper and rockier, and the country far rougher than anything I had seen with Alec MacTavish's brigade. It was a fierce, wild river and it roared down at us, hammered at the canoes, soaked us with icy spray. Lining up the shallows, legs aching with cold, and hauling over the everlasting portages, I wished a hundred times that we could simply turn around, point the canoes downstream and go back. What a ride it would be! But we were going upriver. We made no more than ten miles the first day.

Stumps and slash showed raw where the pines had grown near the river. There were clumps of hemlock and cedars and groves of pine in the distance, but otherwise the woods were drab and leafless. The sky hung whitish-grey and the wind blew raw and chill from the northeast. It snowed and the portages turned slippery and treacherous. My feet were blistered and swollen and my neck and shoulders ached from the pack-sling. The days were short. Toil began and ended in the dark at the narrow, crowded camping places. We slept on the stony ground, half under the canoes, wet and chilled, but so tired that sleep came in an instant. Snow-powdered ice grew along the shore overnight and the river ran black beside it.

It was pure misery, really, but they sang. They humped and hauled and shouted. They drove on and on and they never stopped for a waking moment. And I caught it from them. You had to. No one who complained would last a season in O'Donnell's shanty crew.

Above Rivière la Pêche there was no further sign of cutting. Twelve more miles and we came to Paugan Falls where the river roared down white and wild between ranks of monster pines. Below it on the left was a point of land grown with cedars. Here we landed and camped and we raced against the winter to build the shanty.

14. Rory's Shanty

I lay half-awake one night in late January listening
to the night noises. It was very cold and they were
louder than usual. The crack of a frozen tree
sounded sharp and clear and the wolves' howling
seemed almost at the door. Inside the camboose
shanty, the heavy breathing from the bunks and
the *pop-pop* of the fire were the same as ever, but
the mice seemed noisier. I wondered idly what they
were into with their scratching and whether I had
remembered to sling the sack of peas up out of their
reach. I looked out over my toes to the glow of the
fire in the middle of the camboose. It was much too
comfortable here in my blankets to get up and
check.

    Sunday tomorrow. I curled up warmly. The
men would all lie late in their bunks and Alcide
would fry the salt pork. Every other day of the
week it was boiled in with the peas in the great
iron pot sunk in the sand under the fire. But
Sunday! Sunday was fried pork day. Sunday we
had great slices of it, crisp and delicious and
dripping from the pan. And for supper we had
fried pork again with the fish the gang caught

through the ice during the idle day.

No work on Sunday — except for Alcide Caron and me. Alcide still had to cook breakfast and supper and bake the bread. I still had the wood and the water to haul. I still had to feed that hungry fire. But on Sunday even I could lie in a little longer . . .

Firelight flickered on the low scoop roof. The fire was half curtained-off by the clothes hanging round it to dry. I caught the smell — wet wool, tobacco, sweat and wood smoke and the scent of the tea kettle forever stewing its jet-black brew. The camboose shanty had its own ripe stench — and its own raucous life.

Twenty-four men felling the pine, hewing them square where they lay in the snow, skidding them to the bank of the frozen river. Out in the bitter cold of the Gatineau each dawn they went, and at dark they came stomping back into the camboose, shouting for supper. And there would be Alcide. Tiny Alcide Caron, wiry and toothless with his brown creased old face and his black, shiny, chipmunk eyes and his crumpled nose. He moved in darts and starts, and he danced around the glowing fire like a wizened gnome brewing spells in some shadowed cave. He ruled them all — the *piqueteurs*, the teamsters, the *gars des hâches*, the whole rowdy crew — with a rod of iron. And when supper was done and the axes sharpened and the tall tales began, Alcide would top them all.

The stories he'd told last night — in French which I'd come to understand — tales of the bush and the river, the rafts and the log drives, magic and miracles, canoe brigades and fights, the taverns of Montréal, the ladies of Québec! And then came the sawing of Basile Trudel's fiddle and Alcide leading the dancing and the songs.

Was that the oxen stirring? Odd. I didn't often hear them at night. Their hovels were well behind the camboose. Perhaps everything sounded louder because it was so still and cold. I dozed off.

Someone was moving. Quietly in the snow. Coming closer through the trees. Closer. Shadows lay black in the moonlight.

Indians! I awoke.

Not Indians, of course. I knew now that they weren't bloodthirsty savages. There was Mishen Adawej and his family who trapped in winter well to the north of us. They had been our only visitors — by canoe just before the river closed. They delivered some snowshoes Rory had ordered from Mishen when he was trading down in By's Town in the fall. Mishen spoke mostly French and he knew Rory, Basile and Alcide quite well.

Not Indians, no. I was only dreaming. Or perhaps it was the mice . . .

A stir in the corner woke me again. Someone was getting up, feeling his way past the fire to the door. It opened and closed quietly. Nothing unusual about that. The privy was behind the hovels.

A gentle bump — against the camboose. What was it? I lay fully awake now. Rigid. There was something outside.

The door opened again very gently. The fire flared. It was Alcide. He darted to Rory's corner, then Basile's. I could hear whispers — urgent. He came closer, shook Matthew's feet.

"Quiet, Matt — *lèves, lèves*," he hissed. "Get up. *Vit', vit'*, be quick. Men outside. *Silence!*"

He moved along the line, shaking feet, urging.

Rory was up and dressed, whispering with Basile at the door. The men moved like cats in the dimness, dressing. Not speaking. I pulled on my capote and toque, tied my moccasins.

A handclap, sharp but quiet. I looked up.

Rory O'Donnell's face shone big in the firelight. He held a cant-hook and he raised it over his head. Not a sound. Every eye was on him — every muscle tensed, every man crouched like an animal ready to spring.

He rasped: "Prowlers outside. Must be Burke's boys. When I say the word, grab yerselves something to fight with and get out that door. Half o' yez go to the right with me and half to the left with Basile. Fernand, ye look to the oxen with your men. Matthew, the storehouse with Leo. Alcide, ye stay inside with Marc and Paul and load up them muskets."

A low growl started from the whole pack.

"Out and at 'em boys," quietly. Then —

"Go."

He charged through the door with a roar and the whole gang blundered out behind him into the moonlight, howling like banshees. I was right on Matthew's heels. He swung off towards the storehouse. I slipped and went down in the snow. Someone fell over me, cursing, and the whole gang thundered past my head.

I scrambled up, made for the woodpile, snatched up a club and bounded past the rear corner of the camboose. There in the flooding moonlight were two figures crouched close in to the rear wall. I stopped, looked back. No one with me. I shouted: "Here, Matt — Rory — here they are." At the same time there was a bellow over at the hovels, raging shouts behind me at the storehouse.

The men by the camboose turned towards me, faces white in the moonlight. I yelled again, hurled my club. They turned away, raced ten paces and were swallowed by a snarling wave of our men sweeping round the far corner.

Right where they had been lurking — by the wall — there was a sudden spark and a flare. I bounded forward, slipped, went down, scrambled and dove for the sparks. I smelt burning powder, vaguely saw a length of spluttering fuse, a keg against the logs, a stack of hay.

I reached the fuse, pulled it sputtering from

the keg, flung myself into the snow beyond. A searing pain in my hand, a hissing sound and the fuse was out. I pulled myself out of the snow. Behind me, the barrel lay harmless, the hay unlit. I sat staring at my left hand. There was a black burn right across the palm. I had left my mitts inside.

In a few more minutes it was all over. Lookouts were posted outside with muskets. Marc, Paul and Leo Cronier raced off on snowshoes to scout for any more enemies. We gathered in the camboose and Rory took a quick roll call.

All our men were accounted for. Fernand had been carried back in, unconscious. Matthew had a swelling on his cheekbone and one eye was almost closed. Basile leaned on the post, by the fire, his left arm hanging useless at his side, his face drawn with pain. Alcide slapped a wad of wet tea leaves on my hand and tied a rag around it, then turned to Basile.

We had six prisoners. They had all taken a terrific beating outside in the snow and two of them were barely conscious. They were stretched out on the earth floor with our men standing over them.

Rory jerked his head and the four who could stand were pulled to their feet.

"Now, me buckos, yez'll have some kind of message from Ironbound Burke for his old friend Rory O'Donnell, I'm thinking."

The four — big raw-boned men, Irish by their looks — said not a word.

"Och! Yez think Burke'll come up to help? So he does and he'll get musket balls for his breakfast, bedammit. I notice he didn't have the stomach to come along personal this time, though. Who's in charge of this little party? Must be ye, eh Dooly?"

Rory knew the man. "Come now, Dooly — speak up."

Silence.

"Answer him!" Pat Sullivan chopped Dooly to his knees with a crashing blow on the back of the neck. Dooly glared up at Rory, his mouth set in a tight line.

"Ah!" Rory spat, "take 'em outside a spell boys — and yez can take off their moccasins and their mitts. Keep an eye on 'em. They won't be after goin' far. Meantime, we'll just decide which way we'll get rid of 'em, eh boys?"

There was a rumble of talk around the fire and the prisoners were dragged outside into the cold.

"Well boys," Rory looked around, "yez all did a fine job o' work — includin' young Tom here, pullin' the fuse on that powder. You know, if Alcide hadn't got up to look at the moonlight and seen them louts prowling out there, we'd have been blown up in our bunks. They had powder all set, and hay to burn at the storehouse, and the hovels, too."

Pat spoke up. "Don't know about you, Rory, but I says murderin' swine that does this kind o' thing gets their necks stretched. We've plenty o' rope now, and we're not short o' trees."

"Throw 'em into the Paugan Falls," another voice snarled. "There's enough open water there. Save us the trouble o' cuttin' 'em down and buryin' 'em, eh Pat?"

"Ah, they're all Protestants — no cause to bury 'em — leave 'em for the wolves." Another growl. The men were in an ugly temper. They meant it.

The excitement of the fight had worn off now. But these friends of ours, even they could talk so easily of killing six men — and they intended to do it. It was just a question of how. I felt sick — empty and sick.

I moved over beside Matthew. He spoke, his voice even and cool: "Look now, none of our men is killed. Some hurt, mind, but we haven't lost anyone. If we do away with Burke's men, then in the first place we'll be murderers —" Pat Sullivan snorted scornfully — "and in the second place, Burke will be up here with all the men he can muster for a real battle."

"Let 'em try, just let 'em try," muttered Rory, tight-lipped. "We'll show 'em."

"Now look, Rory," said Matthew, "win or lose the battle, we'll all lose the war — the lumbering, that is. We all want to make our wages out of the winter's work —"

"That's for sure." It was Basile.

Matthew went on: "I say we turn those fellows loose."

"What — what are you sayin', Matt? — turn 'em loose? You're mad!"

"Then turn 'em loose without snowshoes or packs. It's fourteen, fifteen miles to Burke's shanty. Time they make it — if they do — their feet'll be in no shape to work again this winter."

"*Jamais, p't-être.*" It was Alcide. "That will show this Burke he can't beat us. Show him we mean business, eh? He loses the work of six men for the winter and he still has to feed them and pay them. And none of his other boys is going to take the chance against us. Frozen feet — she's a very painful thing. For me, Rory, I think Matt'ew is right."

The faces around the fire showed mixed feelings. Heads began to wag. Talk rumbled.

Rory hesitated only a moment. "Right, boys. Matthew and Alcide and Basile — they have it right — and that's the way it's to be. Pat! All o' yez, now. There'll be no shanty war — unless they comes again. Then — look out! I'll send a personal message to Ironbound Burke with Dooly. Matthew, me boyo, will ye be so good as to write a few words to that slitherin' unholy Orangeman for me. And make a copy of it, too, so that Squire Wright and all them can see we're a peace-lovin' lot. Me own father'll roll over in his grave in old Ireland and it breaks me heart to say it, Matthew, but ye're right."

The scouting party came stamping in the door. Leo Cronier said they had checked all the tracks and none of Burke's men had escaped. Their packs had been found a half-mile down river where they had apparently waited before making their attack. Their snowshoes were by the shore, ready for a fast retreat.

"Bring 'em all in," Rory snapped.

Our men sat around the bunks, the fire on their faces, looking like so many wolves. The six prisoners were dragged in and stood, half-frozen, looking warily around the circle.

"Now, Dooly, me bucko," Rory was smiling, but there was steel in his voice. "Ye hooligans has a long walk ahead o' yez, without yer snowshoes. Ye'll deliver this here letter to Mr. Burke — if ye get there. And I'd advise the lot o' yez to keep on walkin' — if ye've got any feet left to walk on. Any o' yez that my boys sees around the Gatineau or the Chaudière come spring — well — yer life ain't worth a tinker's damn. And that's God's truth."

There was a throaty growl from around the camboose.

"On yer way, now — and a fair good morning to yez all."

Burke's men set off, grim-faced, as the dawn was breaking. It was very cold. They had no snowshoes, no axes, knives or tinder boxes, nothing with them to make camp or light a fire. It was slow, heavy going for them, knee deep in the snow along the river, and it would be deeper in the bush. If they turned back to O'Donnell's shanty, nothing that Rory or Matthew, Alcide or Basile could say would keep the rest from tearing them apart.

The gang sat around with mugs of tea, waiting for breakfast, laughing and joking now; each man telling and retelling his own part in the fight. It had begun to sound like some sort of Waterloo already and it would certainly become another shanty tale to outdo the others in the telling.

Basile's arm was broken. Alcide tied it with a splint and poured him a mug of whisky from the medicine chest.

Rory and Matthew talked and I edged in to listen. "Basile will be all right. Won't be able to do any travellin', though," said Rory, "and I wanted him to go upriver this winter to cruise a new cuttin' area. He's been in there before — built a cabin last year. Didn't have time to cover the whole area, though, or figure how to get the timber out. He says there's pine enough there to make us rich, Matt, and we might be able to get it down another river — and to hell with Burke."

"Why don't I go, Rory?" Matthew asked. "You'll want to stay here yourself, in case of trouble with Burke, I suppose."

Rory screwed up his face and pushed his hair back. "Basile could tell ye how to get there easy enough, I suppose. I can tell ye what to look for.

Don't like to send a new man alone though. Winter's a hard time out in the bush on yer own, Matt, make no mistake about that."

"I could take Tom, then you wouldn't be short any men at the cutting."

There was a pause and Rory tugged at his ear. Then he said: "Right Matt, ye've hit the nail on the head for the second time tonight. Don't know what I'd do without ye." He thumped Matthew on the shoulder. "Look now, me friend — Englishman, Protestant and all — how about being me partner? Between us two we'll fix that black-hearted Burke for fair. We'll talk on it tonight, eh? Look." There was a square of lightening sky at the smoke-hole in the roof. "We'd better get the boys to work squarin' things away."

"Well, boys," he roared. "So much for Iron-bound Burke and his shower o' knaves. We got the muscle and we got the luck, too. And we move fast. Why, another minute and we'd o' had no camboose, no oxen — nor hovels."

"And no storehouse," said Matthew.

"Only the privy," said Alcide, "and it's too small for us all at the same time."

The camboose rocked with shouts and laughter. They echoed and re-echoed through the winter woods for the rest of the day.

These were hard, hard men — these shantymen.

15. Lake of Pines

We left the Paugan Falls shanty as the sun touched the hilltops above the river. The snow had its early morning blue look, and you could see the mist curling up from the base of the falls. There was not a cloud in the sky, not a breath of wind. The men had started cutting by now and I could hear axes and voices crystal clear from deep in the woods. Alcide helped us load up in front of the camboose, and we moved off with our heavy toboggan squeaking and our snowshoes scrunching with that high-pitched sound that comes from the snow when it is very cold.

We turned upriver, heading due north beside the falls. It was steep but quite well packed and I took the second tumpline and helped Matthew pull the toboggan. The trees near the falls were crusted with frost and we toiled up through a feather-white tunnel to the top of the rise. Another hundred yards took us into the stumps and slash of our furthest-up logging area and then the trail sloped down to the frozen river above the falls. There was a stock of huge logs here all set to roll into the water when the ice broke up.

The muffled growl of the falls and the knife-sharp distant sounds of the shantymen at work faded behind us. A jay screamed and flashed blue among the trees. Ahead of us the river stretched away to the north, a smooth carpet of snow-covered ice, hemmed in by steep rock-faces. Cedars clung to them, and hemlocks crowded their tops.

I moved out ahead to break trail for Matthew and the toboggan — breath pluming white, body warm, sweating a little under the pack, mouth and chest tasting the thin cold air, nose ice-cold with the clean smell of winter. The old canoe song ran through my head like a march, beating out the steps:

En roulant, ma boule roulant,
En roulant, ma boule . . .

Snowshoes kicked up the fine-powdered snow, and we swung north mile after mile along the frozen Gatineau.

We skirted, I think, five rapids after leaving Paugan Falls and at the foot of the sixth a smaller river flowed in from the east. Matthew looked at Basile's map and we forked off along it towards a ridge of higher, sharper hills. The sun was low behind us in the west now. The hills ahead glowed pink and shadows lay dark along the river. We dug in and camped for the night.

By the third day we had worked our way up the river, over lakes and trails and now through beaver ponds and meadows, lifting the toboggan over the dams, moving carefully, listening for the sound of running water. Wet feet meant a stop to light a fire and dry them out. Humps of beaver lodges poked their sharp-cut logs untidily through the snow.

We hauled sharply over a narrow trail, well travelled by game, and crossed another pond, another dam. A twisty creek lined with dried brown cattails led us out onto the wide whiteness of Basile's "Lac des Pins." Its far shore was hacked by a high ridge of dome-topped hills, showing bare solid rock, cascaded with ice, too steep to hold snow. The lake was about a mile across and it twisted off in both directions. Above its fringe of cedar the shores were completely clothed in pine.

We turned north along the ice and the miles crawled by.

Through a group of islands and across an open stretch was Basile's red-tinged rock-face. Below it was another narrowing in the lake and there, in the trees, we found his cabin, its scoop roof barely pushing up the snow.

It wasn't much of a cabin — there was no door and we had to clear out the snow — but it was quite tight and there was a sleeping platform of poles and a stone fireplace. After our two nights on the trail, I felt it would do us very nicely. It would be our home for two or three weeks, so we set about making ourselves comfortable.

After supper Matthew got out the map, marked it up with notes on the timber we had passed, distances travelled, details of the route, the beaver meadows, the rivers, the hills.

"Remember, Tom, how we climbed up, little by little, over the dams until we crossed the ridge? Then we worked down a bit and the creek ran into this lake? I would think the outlet is a little further north. Remember Basile said this area was richer in pine than any he'd ever seen? With those steep slopes around the lake it'll be dead easy to cut the lot and skid them down onto the ice."

"Then where do they go?" I asked. "How do you get them over to the Gatineau?"

"We don't. When Basile came in here he reckoned he was over the height of land. This water must flow down into the Lièvre River to the east. The Lièvre runs down into the Ottawa River maybe fifteen miles below the Gatineau. If there's a good clear run from here, or maybe the next lake to this . . . why, don't you see? We could set up shanties next year to cut both sides of the height of land, and drive down both rivers. They'd be close together and we'd have just the one supply line from Wright's. We'd be first to cut in the Lièvre. Why, old man Burke won't even know what we're at. He'll likely waste half his energy working out ways to stop us on the Gatineau, and if we want, we can move all our gangs over this side in no time and we'll control the whole area. What d'you think of that for a plan? It's everyone for himself up here, you know. First in has the timber!"

I said: "Fine, Matthew. It's a fine plan. But . . . "

"But what, Tom? Why, with Rory as a partner . . . "

He looked at me rather strangely, then turned away. The single candle flickered and it was hard to see the expression on his face.

He said: "Tom, I'd better tell you I wrote to Mr. Shirreff before we left Wright's. I told him we'd been offered £2,000 for our land and if he wanted it he should send someone up to O'Donnell's shanty by the tenth of March to make a better offer."

"Two thousand pounds?" I breathed. "Two thousand pounds? Who —?"

"Oh, Jack Snell. He came to see me before we left Wright's. Made an offer."

Made an offer? And he hadn't told me.

"So, when we get back to the shanty we may have bidders with hard cash. Then we can make our decision — sell if we want — and make our agreement with Rory. If we're going to be partners with him, we'll need the money for the double camp next winter, like I said."

He turned to me and his eyes were glowing. "Now you've been up here Tom, seen all the timber, what do you think? It's wealth, boy, right here for the taking. Why, a man only has to be properly organized, have a little capital . . . you understand now, don't you?"

All I could do was shake my head. No! I couldn't part with our land. I couldn't. But Matthew — he couldn't see my way. It was just like that dismal night on the raft. Lumbering had a hold on him. Or was it just quick money? The old Matthew . . .

If this were Father, with his feet rooted in the soil . . .

Partners — and Matthew had said we were partners.

* * *

Matthew spent the next three days from early morning 'til dark working his way through the bush, climbing to high vantage points to survey the timber. Information built up on his maps each night. I cut wood, gathered bark to chink the cabin, set snares and cut fishing holes in the ice. I was alone all day. It was vast and white and cold, but not nearly as deserted as it first seemed.

Morning rounds of my snares usually produced two or three big white snowshoe hares, and an hour or two spent at the fishing holes would bring half a dozen nice grey trout. It had been clear and still and cold for five or six days now, and no fresh snow had fallen. Our food supply grew — a comforting thought, because sooner or later the weather would change.

Birds crowded in on the cabin. The whisky-jacks, big raucous grey jays, found us first and swarmed for scraps whenever I skinned an animal or threw out bones or refuse. Their bluejay cousins watched and shouted. The chickadees were always about in the early morning, calling cheerfully to each other, and the woodpeckers, of course, from the perky, little black and white fellows to the big *"gros pic"* — the size of a crow, with a brilliant red-crested head — dipped and darted through the trees. The clear sharp *rat-tat-tat* of their beaks sounded across the lake.

I carried the musket on my lone snare line rounds, hoping to see a deer or a moose. The weather stayed clear and still. Though I saw tracks aplenty, the animals I spotted were too far off for a shot. I tried to follow them, but after the second day I realized it was pointless in these conditions.

Twice I came across a wolf-killed deer being picked clean by the ravens. It was an ugly, chilling sight and it made me look about for the freshness of the wolf tracks and check the musket's prime. And I kept glancing over my shoulder, half expecting to see a low shadowy form slinking through the trees. Once I could swear I did, and my spine crawled.

On the third evening, after supper, Matthew marked up his map as usual, sucking at his pipe: "I've covered the whole of the lake now, Tom, and a string of ponds and another lake to the south. They all flow this way into Pine Lake." He traced his tracks out on the map. "There's a good-sized outlet up at the north end, though — I haven't been beyond that — but there's quite a drop over a waterfall there and another lake below it. Looks as though it could be bigger than Pine. Seems to lie towards the north between some pretty rugged hills. The outlet could be to the east. The water's got to go someplace. Of course, it might get off to the west and back into the Gatineau . . . or . . . "

He puffed thoughtfully, tapping his finger on the map. "From up top of the ridge you can see lakes and hills wherever you look. And pines, Tom — what pines!" Then: "We've got to find that outlet."

He folded the map away and said: "I'll be off first thing in the morning."

"On your own?"

"Yes, I'll travel light. Don't want a toboggan along. I can manage with a fur and blankets and food for three or four days. Better you stay here, build up the wood supply, and the meat. We'll need it. Why," he chuckled, "you might even shoot a moose! Don't forget you'll have to butcher it in the snow, if you do. And you'll have a little trouble hauling it home. Wouldn't want to get in an argument with the wolves over it, either. Better you stick to deer, Tom. Difficult enough at that."

Matthew left early, striding out past my fishing holes and straight off across the lake. North of the narrows it opened out into an irregular square shape with two rocky islands off on the west side. There was an inlet running off to the north and I could still see his tiny figure moving across the ice in that direction a full half-hour after he left.

Then he was gone and I was alone with the cabin and my thoughts and the hush of the woods.

16. Shadows in the Snow

I opened up my fishing holes with the axe, baited up the hooks with pork fat, then left the fish to catch themselves. The sun was still low and there was a feathery cloud cover glowing pink off in the west. By the time I had brought the night's bag in from the snares, a breeze was blowing across the lake, swirling up clouds of snow. No sign of Matthew now and his snowshoe tracks were beginning to blow in. I found it hard to spot my fishing holes from shore so I cut half a dozen small hemlocks and planted them out on the ice as markers.

It was cold that night. When I brought in wood, the northern lights were leaping high and wild and the stars were sharp as needles. The pines, swaying and whispering fitfully to each other, crowded black behind the cabin. Wolves' cries rose and fell, rose and faded away, echoed and answered, then thinned to nothing.

I banked the fire, made sure of the musket and rolled into my blankets. The fire flickered and crackled. Outside the cold sounds came — the snapping branch, the sudden deep *whoom-whoom-whoom* of the lake ice cracking. And the wolves. They went on and on.

I dreamed of a wolf-torn carcass bloody on the snow, and a man lurking, shadowy, watching me, following.

Daylight brought courage and work chased the dreams from my mind. It was a softer day, not so cold, and the sharp edge was off the distant hills.

In mid-afternoon I spotted a deer on the ice, close to shore, just across the narrows. It was reaching up as high as it could to browse on the cedars hanging out over the lake. The wind gusted in my face now and it sounded in the pines, and I thought I might just be able to get close enough for a shot.

Overhead, the cloud cover had thickened and it was much milder. I went inside quickly and gathered a few strips of dry deer meat, the axe, flint steel and tinder box, powder flask and musket balls. I checked the musket over, tested the flint and primed it. It was already loaded with a heavy ball. I tied on my snowshoes, lashed my axe and pack to the toboggan, settled the tumpline over the hood of my capote and headed down onto the lake with the toboggan trailing light behind me. The deer was still there, its tail twitching white as it fed.

I moved across to the other shore, reached it a hundred yards from the deer, began to work my way gently along under the cedars. I crouched low, stayed in their shadows, moved my snowshoes carefully.

Closer now and the deer hadn't moved. Gently, gently. Almost near enough . . .

A bluejay screeched. The deer turned, head high, ears cocked, and it stood frozen staring straight at me. My heart thumped. It was a long shot. I snapped the musket up to my shoulder, pulled the cock back and took aim. I was shaking, breathing hard. I caught my breath, steadied up, brought the sight right onto the animal's neck. The ears twitched, it shifted, turned its head. I snatched at the trigger, the musket leaped and roared. The deer whirled and bounded off along the shore.

I watched the bobbing white tail in a fury, muttered: "Next time, Penny, squeeze that trigger, don't try to pull it right off, you —"

The shore was steep and the cedar grew thick and the deer stayed on the lake surface until he was about four hundred yards away. I cursed myself again, reloaded and set off briskly, following his tracks. I'd get that deer!

The shadows were rather flat now. The sun showed a pale disk through the overcast, and denser grey-white clouds were gathering. They shed a few fat snowflakes. It was really quite warm and I undid the first two toggles on my capote and lengthened my stride. The tracks led me in under the trees, then up onto the shore. The deer had floundered here, and there was something dark on the snow where it was trampled — a deep red splash of blood.

My heart beat quickly. I had nicked him! I pushed on through the bush for about fifty yards, half running, pulling the toboggan up short behind me. It was heavy going in the deep snow and the deer was in trouble. It showed in his tracks. They led behind a rocky headland, back down onto the snow-covered ice. Then I could see him on the lake again, head down, moving slowly and dragging a front leg. I would have him.

Snow drifted down. The wind had shifted around to the south and east, but my scent didn't matter now. I hurried on, closing the gap. The snow fell more heavily and I lost sight of him. I could see his tracks and, here and there, a splash of blood. I could get to him now. It was just a matter of time. My heart thumped, excitement grew. His tracks stayed close along the shore.

The snow was falling now in big, heavy flakes. On my left, trees loomed dark and to the right, across the lake, there was nothing but a grey-white void. It was dead silent except for the swish of my snowshoes and the toboggan dragging behind. I pushed back my hood and rolled my toque up above my ears so I could hear.

Suddenly, there he was, under a tree. His head showed a little lighter than the darkness of the cedar. I raised the musket, swung my left foot ahead. The snowshoe clacked down on its mate, the deer limped a few paces and disappeared in the whirling snow. Not quick enough.

I would be next time!

I moved ahead, close to the trees, keeping inside his tracks. Out on the lake I could lose myself in the falling snow.

There. Just for a moment. Close. Powdered with snow — almost white — hard to see. He faded before I took aim.

On again, musket ready. A dozen fast steps. There, to the right. Dim, but there. Looming larger. Moving. Yes, solid and dark through the snow. Steady now. Aim, centre it well. Sque-e-eze. Roar, flash, kick, thwack of the ball going home. He sprawled on the snow.

I had him! The deer, that beautiful deer. I jumped, whooped for joy; ran forward, tripped, almost fell in my excitement. There he was. There in the snow.

Now I could see. Now I could see it. My deer. No. Not a deer — not — oh God, no! It was a man. I stumbled forward. A man. Lying there, in the snow. Moving a little. I fell on my knees. I found his shoulders, rolled him on to his side.

It was Matthew.

"Tom. I'm shot — what happened — how did it . . . ?" His voice trailed off. His eyes, puzzled, searched my face. He tried to move. I held him still.

Words caught in my throat. "I — I — It was a deer. I was tracking it — I'd hit it once — The snow — couldn't see properly. Matthew, oh Matthew, I was sure it was the deer I saw. Look over there — see its tracks? There's blood —

Matthew was shaking his head, not looking. Then: "It's my leg. I think — high up — there — somewhere. Ball knocked me over. Don't feel it yet — must be bleeding."

I kicked off my snowshoes and took his off, pulled the toboggan up beside him and managed to roll him onto it. The snow clung to him. I brushed it off and opened up his capote. The trouser leg over his right thigh was wet with blood. Shaking and dry-mouthed, I peeled off my mitts and slit the trousers with my sheath-knife. There was a deep wound on the thigh and it was pouring blood.

Matthew pulled himself up, looked at it briefly and lay back. He said: "Get a bandage on. Tight. Right around, outside the trousers — quick now, Tom. Quick as you can — stop the bleeding."

I half cut, half tore strips from my own shirt, folded a wad over the wound and tied it firmly. The snow was wet and cold, my fingers numb, barely working. Matthew's face told me the pain was beginning and I could feel his body trembling. I peeled off my capote and wrapped it round him, handed him the musket, slipped my snowshoes on and heaved at the tumpline. It took all my weight but I got the toboggan started. The loom of the trees along the shore just showed through the snow.

Twenty paces and I nearly stumbled over my

deer. There it was huddled shaking in the snow. It made a feeble attempt to get up, then fell back, looking at me with enormous, terrified eyes. The snow around it was trampled and packed with tracks. Animals'. There must be other animals near. Just beyond I saw a darkening through the snow, and another, and there — another. Low shapes, crouching, silent, waiting. I stood rigid. They moved closer. There were four of them. Now five.

"Wolves!" I shouted. They ghosted back into the grey. I threw my weight on the tumpline, jerking the heavy toboggan ahead, step by step, fighting panic. Right behind, a snarl. Over my shoulder I could see the whirling snow — a moving shadow, then nothing — nothing more. Snapping now, more snarling. The wolves were at the deer.

It should keep them busy. For how long? How many of them? Could they sense Matthew's wound? They would follow us. How long did we have? Fearful, I sweated on, keeping close to the trees. Listening, looking back. Expecting to see the wolves. Any time now. Any time. I thought of the musket, stopped and knelt beside Matthew. He was rather drowsy.

"I'm all right, boy, I'm all right. Can you make it?"

I nodded: "Look, there's wolves back there. They're at the deer. They might chase us. I'll load the musket. Could you shoot?"

He managed a smile: "I've shot with the odds worse than this, Tom." His lips were cracked and pale. "Yes. Yes, I saw them. If they come after us, you leave me — you hear? You leave me." I said nothing — loaded the musket — gave it back to Matthew — and heaved on.

I lost track of time and distance. The cedars along the shore were my guide, but how far to the cabin? The snow still fell, thick and heavy. I might go right past the narrowing in the lake without seeing the other shore. Then I would miss the cabin altogether. Must stay out from shore as far as I could then, try to see the other side at the narrows. The snow lay deeper now and the toboggan came harder and harder behind me.

Each step became a major move. Get set, stoop against the line, knees bent, then heave ahead. One step forward. Then get set and heave again. Two feet at a time. The greyness went on and on. The faint trees on my right changed shape vaguely, otherwise I could have been standing still in my grey-white silent world. It was late now. The sky was duller.

No sound from Matthew. No stirring. He lay very still, powdered with snow.

Should I leave him? Scout ahead? Perhaps cut out from shore, look for the narrows and the cabin? I could move quickly without the load. If I lost sight of the trees though I could wander in circles on the lake. Surely I couldn't be too far from the cabin. Had I overshot? The falling snow was thick as fog and it was getting dark.

I looked back. The wolves — the wolves were there somewhere in the snow. Had they finished the deer? My own breath came harsh and loud. I held it, listened. No sound in the snow-wrapped silence.

I leaned on the line, barely able now to move the load. I heaved on, fighting panic, fighting the urge to run off blindly through the snow.

Shadows seemed to move now, half-seen. Darker, dimmer. Coming closer. Matthew on the sled. I couldn't leave him. He had told me to, but now, how could I?

There. Right ahead. A dark smudge through the snow. Another to the right — and beyond, another. The wolves. Gently I stepped backwards to Matthew. They were still there. I took the musket. His eyes flickered, but he hardly moved. I peered ahead again, crouched beside him, musket ready.

They were there. Motionless shadows. There — waiting. I cupped my mitts, shouted. It was only a rasp. I shouted again. Still there. No movement.

Now, raise the musket. Cock it. Only one shot. Careful aim now. Squeeze . . .

Clack! The cock snapped forward. No powder flash. No shot. Wet prime. I cursed in despair, blinked away the snow, fumbled with the musket. Ahead they were still there. No movement.

I looked again. That blot. That nearest blot in the snow. It was a tree. A tree, growing on the ice. On the ice?

My fishing hole markers. My little hemlocks. Not wolves. My own markers. I knew how their line lay. They would lead me to the cabin. I knelt there, shaking, gathering strength. We were nearly there.

Somehow I got Matthew up the steep bank and into the cabin, stripped and wrapped in blankets. He was cold — cold to the bone and pale as the snow. I stirred the fire, rubbed him, fed him tea, moved heated stones from the fireplace into the blankets. Gradually his teeth stopped their chattering, his trembling eased. The pain was there. I could see it in his eyes.

He muttered: "My fault, Tom. Coming back . . . across . . . the lake. Snowing. Started snowing . . . lost my bearings. Accident, Tom . . . accident. Don't worry. Good fellow. Thanks . . . thanks."

17. Death's Door

Matthew lay listless and in great pain for two days. The snow continued. It got much colder again and a harsh wind blasted fine grains of snow through slits in the cabin. There was enough firewood at the door and rabbits and fish inside to keep us going for a few days.

The firelight flickered endlessly. I watched him lying there. His face seemed to sink almost to a skull and I could only just hear his breathing. I hardly dared go out or even sleep, with him as he was. I got a few mouthfuls of broth into him whenever he was conscious and I kept him as warm as I could.

The wound was ugly. It oozed continually and there was a massive bruise over his whole thigh. Our "medicine chest" held some bandages and a flask of whisky. I washed the wound with the whisky and kept clean bandages on it, but if anything, it seemed to get more fiery.

Late on the second night he began to stir and turn in his sleep. By morning he was hot, sweating and shivering with fever. When I stripped off the bandage his thigh was dark red, hard and hot to the touch — much more swollen than before — and the skin was stretched tight. I put a hot compress on the wound, left him with some tea to drink and went outside.

The sky was clear, but the fine-blown snow and the bitter north wind made the going hard. It took me a very long time to do what I had to — set some snares, chop open some fishing holes, bait the hooks and bring in a few logs. My eyes streamed in the wind and the lids froze together. By the time I was back inside, one cheek and the side of my nose had frozen hard.

Matthew's fever grew higher. His face was drawn and flushed and his eyes seemed to have sunk deep into their sockets. The wound smelled putrid now and the swelling was worse. He was barely able to take a spoonful of tea through his dry, cracked lips.

He looked up at me. He must have seen despair on my face for he made a huge effort, raised himself, motioned to me to prop him up. I placed a couple of short logs and a folded blanket behind his back.

His voice croaked: "Show me, Tom." I took off the bandage. He felt around the wound, then shook his head. "Poisoned. I've seen it before. Smelled it, too. Army sawbones would cut a man's leg off for less."

He looked at me for a long moment. Then: "Have to do something, Tom, or I'm done." He tried a smile. "You'd have a little trouble burying a fellow in that frozen ground, eh? Easier if you'd been a better shot, boy — or left me for the wolves."

"What can I do, Matthew?" I stared helplessly at the dreadful leg. "I — I'd go for help, but it would take days. I can't leave you . . . "

"No sense. I'd be finished before you got back, anyway. That ball is still in there. Got to try to get it out. Maybe then the poison'll drain. Think you can be a surgeon, Tom? You've got a strong stomach . . . be as good as plenty I've seen in my time. You won't be drunk, leastways . . . most of 'em are. Get me some water, will you?"

A surgeon! I looked helplessly about. What did we have for surgeon's tools? How could I cut into—? I looked down at the terrible wound again. The thought made me gag.

He moistened his cracked lips, managed a smile. "I can tell you what to do. Helped the surgeon and his mates many a time. Had a ball in me at Waterloo, you know. Once you start, Tom, you've got to go on to the end, though, no matter what. I'll make a noise about it too, because it's going to hurt. I'll swear, curse at you, call you all sorts of names. But Tom —" He gripped my wrist, sat up straight and looked hard into my eyes. "Tom, if you can do it," his voice was quiet and steady now, "if you can do it, then I think I've a chance."

He didn't need to say the rest — if I couldn't do it then he would die. It was as simple as that.

My mouth was too dry to speak. I could only nod my head.

"Good lad." He lay back and closed his eyes a moment. The wind sighed in the pines, whistled close around the cabin. Then he went on quite briskly: "First you fill the kettles up and boil them."

I set the water to boil.

"Now, sharpen up your knife." I found the stone and began to hone my sheath knife. It was a clumsy, wide-bladed weapon.

"Get mine ready too, Tom. Better steel. Holds its edge. Heavy, though. Made for skinning moose, not people. And you'll want needles. You'll stitch it up after. Through the skin, both sides — like this . . . "

I went on with the grisly preparations, straining to remember every word. I poured a mugful of whisky and set it aside, then handed Matthew the flask. He started to drink from it in steady sips.

Strips of shirt for bandages, swabs, the mug of whisky, needles threaded with coarse linen, the kettle-full of hot water with the two sharpened knives standing in it — all my crude surgeon's tools were laid out on the log table. I built the fire up and lit all the candles. I searched the cabin and my mind for something more to make ready.

Matthew handed me the near-empty flask. "Save the rest for a celebration, Tom." He was almost jaunty. His face was flushed and his tongue a little thick. The whisky was taking effect. It would deaden the pain for him a little.

What else now? I looked at the awful leg, then at the knives. Sharp as they were, and however careful I was, they would do brutal damage. I should have something much finer.

"Now tie me down, Tom. Right across my chest. Yes. I mean it, lad. The tumpline will do. And my knees and ankles. Wrists around the poles, there. So I can't lash out at the surgeon, you know. Might give you a black eye. That's right. Watch your knots, there, sailor, don't want them to slip."

The wind moaned, probed the cabin, and the candles guttered. Lashed to the bunk, Matthew lay still, his face drawn and flushed, waiting. My palms were sweating and my knees felt like water. The monstrous knives were a horror. How could I ever handle the task at all, much less with these?

Matthew muttered: "I'm ready, Tom — you set?"

"Yes." I said. I looked down at him. The light flared and fell. There was a deathly silence — not even the winter sounds or the wind.

He said very clearly: "God bless us both. Go to it, boy. Go to it."

I made a quick, firm cut across the face of the wound. He tensed, but he held still and I cut again.

The world hushed to a stop and I saw nothing, sensed nothing but the wound, the flesh, the blood and the knife. I cut, probed deep, opened the wound, swabbed and probed again. Deep down the knife point found the ball. Matthew tensed, gasped in pain. I cut back a little, helped with the other knife, feeling the ball, working it upwards. Matthew arched against the ropes, straining, silent, hands clenched, jaw clamped. Blood flowed. I worked on. I had it now. I had it!

Out! The ball flipped out, rolled, dropped to the earth floor, bloody. I stared stupidly, dropped the knives on the table.

A sigh. Matthew lay limp and quiet. Unconscious. The wound, rushing now. Black blood, liquid, poison. Yes, this was right. Hot swabs. Heat to draw the poison. Clean it up. Bleeding slowing down. Whisky now, wash it well. The needle. Clumsy fingers. Jabbing. Stitches, crude but strong enough. Gently pulled tight. Gently — leave an opening for the wound to drain. More whisky and a clean, dry bandage. Cover him up. Keep him warm.

I stared at my hands in sudden horror. They were dark with blood.

Prickling with sweat, stomach heaving, I lurched through the door into the cold. I leaned there, half-crouched against the wall: retching, quaking, sobbing with relief and fear together; gulping the clean, thin, icy air; rubbing my hands i͏ the snow — rubbing, rubbing, rubbing them clean.

I stood trembling then, my head lying back weakly against the logs. A million stars glittered in the blackness. The lake stretched away, silver-white to the dark hills beyond. The cold pierced to my bones.

It was done.

Morning came. He was weak and hollow-eyed, but the fever was down and his leg was cooler.

He thanked me quietly. "Not many could have done what you did, Tom."

I remembered where the ball lay, picked it up and dropped it in his hand.

"How do you feel?"

"Better, I think — better. I don't remember much. The whisky helped, I suppose."

He drank a little tea. "Look, Tom," he said. "I'm not out of the woods yet. I've got a chance with that ball out now, but I won't walk for a while. Not 'til after break-up. Then the only way out will be by canoe." His voice trailed off.

Without much hope, I said: "Maybe Rory and the boys will come looking for us?"

He shook his head.

"I'll go get them, then." I said.

Preparations took the rest of the day. I stacked the cabin with firewood, did the rounds of my snares and fishing holes. With a real stroke of luck I shot a deer, butchered it and hung the

pieces in the cabin. I extended the sleeping platform so he could crawl over and feed the fire. I
left the musket, powder and shot close by.

Then in the morning I slung up my pack. "Six
days, Matthew, with a little luck from the
weather. I'll be back." I tried to sound cheerful.

Matthew gripped my hand and looked
straight at me from his sunken eyes. "You're a
man now, Tom, and you're on your own. Look. If
I'm not here — when it comes to deciding on our
land — well — maybe you've made your own
decision already — but wait a bit, Tom. Talk to
Squire Wright about it. Get his advice. He's a
good man . . . "

He never expected to see me again. I could
see it in his eyes when he said good-bye. I tried
to say it, too, but no words came.

I walked out into the glittering cold and
across the vast bleakness of the lake. I told
myself there was a hope — if I moved fast.

It was faint, but it was still a hope.

18. Alone

The days were longer now, with a little warmth in the sun. I wound up the frozen creek at the head of Pine Lake and crossed the pond. Its fringe of dried brown cattails poked sadly through the snow. Then over the beaver dams and the ponds and meadows beyond. Dead topless trees stood grey and forlorn. It was a sad and ugly place and deathly quiet.

On across more dams with the faint warning sound of water running beneath the snow. A lake to cross, crowded close with cedars; another creek, a bigger lake, an untrod portage path through dark hemlocks by a frozen rapid to another lake; and on and on and on.

The sun sank lower, the rocky hills above glowed pink. Trees laid long shadows in the snow; pools of blackness gathered by the shores. Moving shadows lurked a shade beyond my sight. Were all the sounds my own? How many times did I look behind? How many miles did I hum away, or whistle half-breathless to break the hush? How many times did I stop in mid-stride to listen — and hear only my own breath?

Night pulled in and I dug my lair in the snow,

heaped its floor with balsam, rigged my lean-to and lit a fire. The light and the warmth made a tiny circle of safety. Beyond it lay the endless dark, the blackness of the pines against the stars, the leaping weirdness of the northern lights and the wild rising voices of the wolves.

It was snowing gently in the morning and milder and I moved on down the winding river. Shadowy fears still chased me, but the day ran its course. I reached the Gatineau and dug in for the night on a bluff, just upstream from a portage path and the top of an open rapid. One more day and I would be at the shanty. With people. I had managed. I had moved along, in spite of fear, and cold, and the forest. I could make it now. I crouched by the fire and ate, and I slept like the dead.

A jay called harsh and urgent in the first of the morning light and I awoke. The river was still deep in shadow. Chickadees moved close in as I stirred the fire and heated the mess of peas left frozen in the pot. Their cheerful *dee-a-dee-dee* won them a handful of dried peas from the bottom of my bag. They were welcome company and their perkiness cheered me. I ate and drank my tea, more confident now, and I looked at the day.

The snow had stopped and it had cleared but the sky was curled with high ferns of wispy cloud. The weather might not hold. My pack was stowed and ready, my axe still bedded in the tree above my head, snowshoes upright in the snow. A last mug of tea from the kettle now — hot and bitter — before moving off.

The jay again, screeching in the stillness. The sun edged over the hills and caught the river below. The snow glowed golden and the mist rose ghostly white from the blackness of the open water, downstream, above the rapid. The cedars there were crusted white with frost. No sound. Deadly quiet.

Then a crunch, a distant squeak.

A clack, as a snowshoe sometimes sounds — a man. No animal, no bird or river sound, that. It was a man.

Someone was coming up the portage trail. Someone else travelling in the bush. Rory? Men from the shanty? Indians perhaps? Anyone — oh — anyone. I shook with relief and I cupped my mitts around my mouth, filled my lungs with ice-cold air, shouted "Halloooo —"

"Hallooooo — hallooo —"

It echoed back from the other shore, then down from the hills and faded. The sounds along the trail stopped, then started again. A little quicker? I thought so. No other sound, only the snowshoes. I fuelled the fire, dug out more tea from my pack.

And there he was.

He swung out of the shadowed portage and down onto the river — a big man, hunched under his pack, his hood up. I could see the axe handle and the musket barrel poking up above his head.

His breath plumed white. Not an Indian — too heavy, too awkward on his snowshoes.

He saw the smoke from my fire, paused a moment, waved a hand. I could see a fringe of frost on his beard. Head down, he paced the last fifty yards. He was just below me and turning up the slope to my camp when I knew who he was.

Rooted, I watched him moving closer. He laboured up the last few steps, saw me at the fire, stopped, legs astride. He sucked a long breath in through his teeth. His eyes narrowed. The frosted beard moved with a twisted grin.

His hand reached slowly up to his hood, pushed it back from his head. A cold hand tightened around my heart.

He said: "Well, as I live and breathe! If it ain't me old shipmate, Tom Penny!"

Dirk Black.

"Been a while, eh Tom?" He swung his pack down and bent to take off his snowshoes.

"Well, well, you got a fanny o'tea on the fire. All ready for old Dirk, eh lad? Now a drop o' that'd go right well. Don't mind if I sits down to join you? Nice surprise meeting an old shipmate way out here — all on our lonesome, like." He stepped towards the fire, half-smiling as though we were old friends.

I said: "What do you want, Black?"

Whack! He caught me a sudden crashing blow on the face with the back of his mitt. It jolted me flat onto my back in the snow. He sneered down at me. It was the same Dirk Black, deadly, vicious, quick as a cat. The beard was new, nothing else had changed.

"Now, now, Tom! That's not a nice way to talk. You just pour me a fresh mugful o' that tea there, and don't try any of those old tricks o' yourn. You're all alone so you might just as well be civil."

I picked myself up, watching him carefully, and filled my mug from the kettle. He took it from me, pulled a flask from his pack and added a tot of whisky. Then he drank, added more whisky and sat back. "Ah, that's better. Hard for a honest rum-drinking sailor-man to get used to this here whisky, Tom, but a nice drop o' tea along of it helps get it down."

He was still grinning at me and his teeth showed yellow against the edging of frost on his beard.

"Now then, let's get down to it. Where's your Uncle Matthew?"

"What do you want with him?"

He moved, as though to hit me again, but for some reason he held off. He settled back on his haunches by his pack.

"Well, seein' as I came all this way to see the two of you, I might just as well tell you — then you'll take me along to him and we can do our little bit o' business, all happy and friendly like." He stopped to drink.

"Ye see, Tom, I wants to buy that land o' your uncle's, and I got the money." He patted his pack where it lay in the snow. "Someone told me Matthew Penny would sell for £2,000 if he hadn't got a better offer from Shirreff and his lot. So up the river I comes to O'Donnell's shanty, and I carried the mail to them from Wright's Post Office, too, I did, and they tells me where to find your cabin. 'Up the Gatinoo,' they said, 'and haul round to starboard past the fifth rapid' — and here we are."

"Why do you want our land?"

He shrugged. "Shirreff wants it, don't he? Canals. That's his idea. Could be mine, too. What's it to you? I'm here with the money and you Pennys got the land. Just a business deal, Tom — between old friends. Right?"

"We won't sell."

"Won't sell? For £2,000? You won't sell? You're daft, you are. Why keep it? You'll never build a canal."

"It's our farm, that's why," I shot back.

"Your farm," he sneered. "I never seen it but Jack said you Pennys picked the wrong lots if you want to farm. Look — 2,000 would buy you four times the land you got there. Much better land, too, with plenty of money left over. So you could have your cake and eat it."

"Jack? — Jack Snell? You know him?" I glanced back down the empty trail.

"Lots of questions, haven't you?" He took a pull at the mug. "No, he's not with me. If you must know, me old mate Jack, he clewed up in the river where it's open, just below the Chaudière. Frozen stiff. Serves him right, mind. Turned out to be a proper rogue, Jack did." He shook his head and clucked his tongue mockingly. "Why, he got hold of the key to Colonel By's strongbox — where he keeps all the money for the canal work, you understand. Jack opened it up and pinched the bank notes. Didn't take much coin. Too heavy. You know, I think he'd have got clear away to Montréal and beyond if he'd cut me in and if he hadn't happened to fall over the bridge. Very careless of him. They never did find the money, either. Seems it must have gone under the ice." He shook his head again and rolled his eyes upwards. "Poor old Jack!"

"So now, Mr. Black, you just happen to have lots of money."

He laughed. "You pick things up quick, Tom. That's what I like about you — quick." His face turned dark. "Ah, don't waste any prayers on Jack — he was a bungler. Had all sorts of great ideas, mind, and nothing against slitting a throat or two, so long as there was plenty in it for him. But you couldn't depend on him. Soldiers is all the same. No sir, Jack were soft, really. When it come right down to it, he didn't ever really finish off a job proper. Here — a little tea for your old mate."

He held the mug out for more, topped it up with whisky and took a long pull.

"Ah, that's the stuff for a bright winter's

morning." His words were light, almost friendly, but there was a knife-edge of menace behind them, and his eyes never left me. He wiped his mouth with the back of his mitt.

"No sir. If it hadn't been for Jack, you know, we'd have got the whole job done neat and tidy a year ago, back there in Portsmouth — made our profit and stayed in merry old England, 'stead o' coming out here to this God-forsaken colony. Still — all's well that ends well. There's all the more for me now, with Jack out o' the way. He won't get his share and neither will that rotten little Twiss."

Twiss! What was this about? Black knew Twiss! And Snell — in Portsmouth? How were they all connected? What did he mean by "share"? His tongue was wagging from the whisky. I must keep him talking.

I ventured: "I didn't like Twiss. He tried to buy our land for £500. For someone else, he said. Just after Father . . . died."

Black snorted: "Another bungler, he was. Bad as Jack. Sneaky, too. Why, d'you know he tried to bargain with Jack and me for half the take? Half! When it weren't his idea in the first place, and he weren't taking none of the risks nor doing any of the — ah — dirty work, you might say."

What was he talking about? He watched me over the rim of the mug, his eyes narrowed into slits, reading the bafflement on my face. He frowned, lowered the mug, pursed his lips.

"You do know who killed your father, don't you?"

His face worked under the beard in a twisted grin and his breath came loud, like an animal panting.

I shook my head. His eyes burned into mine.

"You don't know?"

My head still shaking, I said, "No."

"Hah!" Black tossed his head and snorted. "Well, you might as well know the truth for all the harm you can do — so you can see what a dolt you really are. And so's you'll give credit where credit is due."

He leaned towards me, lips parted, and his voice rasped. "It was me — Dirk Black. Me, with a little bit o' help from Jack Snell."

"You —" I heard my own voice cry out.

He sat back and rocked on his haunches, eyeing me with a kind of vicious delight as though he had stabbed me already and was watching me writhe my life away.

"Quite a tale it is too. Quite a tale. It was Jack Snell as got wind of the land business, you know. He was out here first off with the Sappers and Miners to work on the Rideau Canal. Got to know people hereabouts. He was going back to England with despatches, so Mr. Shirreff asked him could he get hold o' those lots by the Chats Falls afore they were granted out. Promised him a thousand pounds. Happened Jack sailed over in the *Southdown* and we gets to talking. Well, soon's we gets to Portsmouth, we sees Mr. Leech's advertisements for the land grants. Jack goes to see him and meets Twiss, but he hadn't got the maps yet."

He took another drink.

So, the big corporal on the stairway at Mr. Leech's chambers — it was Snell. That's where I'd seen him before. Black's eyes glittered, and held mine like a snake's. He licked his lips.

"We talks the whole thing over with Twiss that night at the Boar and we sees all you Pennys looking over the maps. Twiss has a try but he can't see what lots you're minding to choose, so Jack and me, we waits around next afternoon. Twiss listens to all the talk in Leech's office and he nips out and tells us quick as a wink that you're taking exactly the lots that Shirreff wants. So we sees what to do. If we gets rid of William and Matthew Penny — right away before they can get out to Canada — the two lots will go back for granting to some other old soldiers or sailors. Jack and me can put in for them and Twiss will see we gets them. Free, of course. We'll slip Twiss £100 for his trouble and we'll sell to Mr. Shirreff for £1,000. Just as easy as that."

He laughed, a short, cold laugh.

Just as easy as that! Just kill Father and Matthew and collect £1,000 — easy as snapping your fingers! All I could do was stare at him in horror. He sat there, his mitts around the mug, his lips parted in an evil sneer. He was enjoying this. He was mad.

"Took us a while to finish off your father — fought like a tiger, he did. And that Snell. Panicky. Said he heard someone coming. Job only half done. Had to finish it on my own. I did. Told you Jack was a bungler, didn't I! Like when we'd laid out Matthew Penny after — that was another Snell bungle. Swore he'd cracked his head for good and all. We went through his pockets — make it look like robbery, you know. But Jack didn't hit him hard enough. Want a job done right, do it yourself I always say."

He tipped his head back and drained the mug and wiped his mouth with his mitt. "Then your Uncle gets off to Canada before we has another crack at him. Your Mother won't sell to Twiss, so we fix up passages for you on the *Southdown* and make it look like Mr. Leech arranged it. Easy. So all I had to do was cozy up to Widow Penny. Maybe I could marry the land." He laughed suddenly. "If that didn't work I'd feed you both to the sharks on a dark night and go after Matthew. Dirk Black don't give up easy."

He looked at me with grim satisfaction. "So here we are, Tom Penny. Here we are."

19. Last Encounter

He stood up, stamped his feet and thumped his mitts against his ribs.

" 'Struth! This place is colder'n the hubs o' hell! Let's get moving now, Tom. Got to see Matthew Penny. You're going to show me the way nice and helpful like, ain't you?"

Without really caring what I was saying, or what he might do to me I said: "You can find him yourself."

He started towards me and his face darkened. Then it cleared and he bared his teeth in a vicious grin. Squatting beside his pack, he fished out his whisky flask again and drank — watching me, eyes never leaving my face. Silence. I could feel my heart beating, my throat tightening with fear.

He could beat me, try to make me lead him to the cabin. But Rory had told him the way already so he didn't really need me — except — yes of course, to twist a signature out of Matthew. If the money didn't work he could use a threat to my life to get that signature. Then he could simply kill us both. And he didn't know that

Matthew was already half dead. He didn't know how easy it would be.

If I could slip away — get down to the shanty. One day there, three days back up to the cabin with Rory to help . . . I'd be too late.

"Aye lad. You're right. Now you mention it. I could find him myself — easy. With all what the boys at the shanty told me." He pulled at the flask again. "So you're about as much use to me as a pound o' tea. Maybe I'd just like your company, though. So, you break camp. And remember, Tom —" his eyes had that wild glitter again, "one step out o' line and I'll kill you." He let the words sink in. "Slow — very, very slow. . . . Oh yes, and I'll have your knife." He pointed to my sheath knife, then to the snow at my feet.

I drew the knife and dropped it, then squatted at the fire for my kettle. It was still boiling. He moved towards me, huge and evil, looming dark against the sky, mittened hands ready . . .

His breath rasped, hung white in the stillness. He stooped near me. I could smell the whisky. Now. His eyes on the knife, my mitts around the kettle.

A bluejay flashed close, screamed.

NOW!

My hands flung upwards. The boiling tea took him full in the face. He shrieked, clapped a mitt to his eyes, swung with the other hand, groping. I rolled under, snatched my knife from the snow, leaped clear.

Snowshoes — on in seconds. Now — the river. A raging bellow behind, a snarling face, eyes seeing now, coming hard.

I ran, toes up, kicking snow. Through the trees and down, down. Too slow. Can't go faster. Might trip. Sinking down the slope now. Deep, deep snow. Don't fall. Don't fall! A rasping curse behind.

On the river now, level, snow firmer. A glance back. He was part way down the slope, waist deep, floundering. He stopped, turned back, half dragging himself up by the trees. Going for his snowshoes. Now I had a start.

I ran out from the bank and downstream, snowshoes swinging up and ahead, up and ahead in a pounding rhythm, flying over the flat, sparkling snow. Breath came hard and cold and steady. I had a hundred yards' start. A shout from behind and I glanced back. He was down on the river now, on his snowshoes, stumbling, but moving fast. And he had his musket.

Oh God! His musket! My heart thumped wildly. I drove on, feeling fear now, weakness in my legs.

Ahead, the trees were laced with frost. The mist hung over the open water. I could get by on the other side. But then? The banks grew steep and the river narrowed. Then the rapid. The place, the one place I might have an edge. I slowed, stole a glance behind. He was coming steadily, a little closer. My mind was clear now, panic gone, thinking fast. This would be the place. Yes, here on the river. When would he try a shot?

Go on. Go on! I forced myself ahead. Ran, tried to judge the distance to the open water. I began to jig like a rabbit. Running, running, running. The water close ahead was black against the snow. My snowshoes dragged.

Legs of lead, breath coming in sobs, a taste like blood in my mouth, I slowed, turned. He was fifty yards behind. On again, slower, dragging now. Another look. Thirty yards — and he had stopped, aiming. I spurted ahead, dodging, leaped aside.

The masket crashed. A gigantic blow on my shoulder and I toppled forward, rolled, struggled to my knees, half facing him, tried to breathe.

A great mad shout exploded across the snow. He stood there, the musket smoking in his hand, head flung back, laughing wildly. The dreadful sound rolled across the river, echoed back from the rocks, then back and back again. Higher and higher it rose 'til the river rang with a wild crazed shriek.

I crouched watching. Mitt off, my hand in my pocket groping for my knife. He moved closer. Twenty paces. Closer he shambled. Closer. Ten paces. I had it now, had it in my hand. Hard and cold.

Up! I moved straight for the black open

water. He was right behind.

Water now, under the snow. Darkening it. Clogging my snowshoes with slush. Weighting them like lead. Legs — in a nightmare — barely moving.

Close to the dark edge. Turn alongside it. This is the place. Now is the time. Now.

Stop!

Turn. Face him. Knife out. Arm extended.

He stopped, eyes on it, wide. We stood a frozen instant. I lunged. He reared back, brought up the musket, struck at the knife.

Then the ice gave. It crumbled as I knew it would. Water swept my feet, ice-cold.

Fear on his face then. He sank through to his knees, flailing, and he screamed. I lunged for firm ice, splashed, scrambled, felt it give, felt the shock of the water. I rolled, squirmed, clawed. It held. I rolled and rolled again.

Then I looked back. His head and shoulders still showed above the water. His arms were spread on the breaking ice. His eyes stared wide with terror and he whimpered: "Help me, boy. Help me — please —" and his head sank lower and the ice broke and floated away in chunks on the slick black water, down to the rapid below.

He thrashed for a moment and he was gone.

I lay sobbing, spent, wet to the waist, cold seeping into my bones. But I had done it. It had worked. Black was gone. We were free of him. If

I could just go on to the shanty. A day's walk. Just a day.

A little rest first, though. Here, on the snow. So tired. So terribly tired. But I'll have strength to move — soon. In a little while.

Move, Tom. Now! If you lie in the snow you'll die. Get back to the camp. The fire. The fire is still burning. Get back to the camp. There was a growing fiery pain in my left shoulder. Black's musket ball.

I got to my knees, to my feet — lurched forward. A step, another, another. Snowshoes, moccasins, trousers — all so heavy — laden with ice. Frozen. Rigid. Too much, too much for me to lift. I clumped a few steps; fell, crawled — face in the snow, arms sinking deep. Pain in my shoulder. The snowshoes dragged, held me. Must get them off.

Cut them. The knife.

I pulled my right hand from the snow. It was bunched in a fist, and it was white, dead white. Frozen. No feeling. No movement. Useless.

But the knife was there held rigid in my frozen hand. I hacked at the ice on my legs, tried to cut the snowshoe thongs. Too hard, though. The ice was too hard, my hand too clumsy.

Get on to the camp then, to the fire.

In a minute. In a minute. Lie here a little first. Rest a bit. I'm not so cold now. Nothing hurts any more, and it's soft in the snow. Almost like lying in long fresh grass.

I remember, so long ago, at Edgeham. In the spring. The sun was warm then, warm and soft, and the new grass smelled so good. And life was peaceful. Then . . . one by one. Father, then Mother, now me. Most likely Matthew next.

Strange to come to an end, here on the frozen river. Alone. I'm sorry, Matthew, sorry I couldn't make it to the shanty. If only I could have a few words with you. Just a few words. About the farm. I'd sell it now. I would. Really . . . Strange. We really could have bought much better land with the money. A better farm for the Pennys. And money left over. For you, Matthew, to put into lumbering if you wanted. Sensible. Father would have done it. I've been blind and stubborn. But it's too late, now. Too late to tell you that . . . too late . . . And Will. Poor Will. He'll be alone now. The last of us.

Alone.

20. Winter's End

It seeped into my mind that some silent, dark people took me with them, that they warmed me and worked over my frozen feet and hands. Then I dreamed of torture. It started with a tingling in my toes and fingers, like the jabs of red-hot needles and it grew and spread until a million of them stabbed me to the bone. I told them to let me die. The pain was too much. But it was a dream and I couldn't make them understand.

It was dark for a long time then, and light again with sun in my eyes, then dark. The pain came pulsing like the tide — growing, piling wave upon wave to a dreadful peak. Then it would turn and ebb away and dwindle gently into the dark and I would sleep. But it would come again and again and again. Dream piled on dream and merged with the pain and the dark into a hideous spun-out nightmare. . . . Next, I remember an odd sound. It was a steady drumming and it went on and on. For a long time I lay in darkness with the sound filling my ears. Gradually it came to me. Rain. It was rain. Rain beating on a roof. Steady heavy pounding rain.

There were other sounds behind it, too. Faint sounds. Somehow familiar — and a smell that I knew.

My eyes were open. The glow of a fire touched the underside of a low scoop roof. I lay there wondering and watching as a faint square of light above me got slowly lighter.

The smoke hole. It was no dream. This was the camboose. Rory O'Donnell's shanty.

I lay on my back watching morning come and I hurt. My hands and my legs ached and throbbed and when I moved a pain stabbed my shoulder.

There was a stirring around the fire. Its light flared up. Voices muttered. I tried to call out, but nothing came. Tried again. A croak, just a croak. The rain drowned it. My lips were dry and cracked. Another try. Still a croak but louder.

Someone moved towards me with a candle, shadows leaped high. Then the light caught his face — round and shiny with a big nose and a lock of hair down over his forehead.

Rory O'Donnell. Behind him was Alcide Caron's weathered face.

Rory's voice. "Did I not tell ye these Pennys was tough enough? Alcide? Look at him, smilin' already."

I tried to talk. They gave me sweet tea, holding the mug for me. I cleared my throat and tried again. I hurt dreadfully, but I was alive and with friends. I didn't know how — but I was alive.

Matthew! I tried to say his name. "Matthew."

It was just a rasp in my throat and Rory was talking. "Half frozen and three-quarters dead, ye was. Lying out on the ice there. Fell in, eh? What's that? Oh yes. Mishen Adawej. The Indian ye know, and his family. They found ye. Brought ye in. Near dead, like I said. Frozen hands and feet. Mishen said the tracks showed ye'd had a fight with a big white man. He went through the ice. That Dirk Black, was it? They brought in his pack along with yers."

But Matthew! I struggled to sit upright and knocked the mug away.

"Matthew." I rasped. "He's up there. Hurt. I shot him. He's bad. Got to go. Now. We've got to go and get him, Rory."

"Go? Can't go anywhere now, laddo. Hear that rain?" He tossed his head upwards. "Early spring. Snow's rotten — ice is too. The oxen and the sleighs went downriver a week ago. Just the drive crew left here now. Ye've been out a long time, Tom. Can't travel anywhere now 'til the rivers open."

My heart sank. Alcide ducked back into the gloom.

Rory said: "Now this Dirk Black. What was the ruckus between the two o' yez?"

"He killed my father, Rory — in Portsmouth. And he tried to kill Matthew too — for our land — he wanted our land. He'd have killed Matthew for sure up at the lake. Me too, probably. I just had to get him out on the ice where it would break. It was the only thing I could do. But now — Matthew — we'll be too late. Rory. He'll —"

Pain shot suddenly up my legs and I had to clamp my teeth and screw my eyes tight shut.

A voice said gently. "Tom. You did everything a man could do." It was a voice I knew so well. "Thank you — partner."

I opened my eyes and there was Matthew Penny, half-carried by Alcide and Basile Trudel.

They eased him down onto the end of my bunk. His face was drawn and gaunt and grey, but his eyes shone.

"Matthew!" I half shouted. "How —?"

"Oho!" Rory broke in with a hoot. "Tom now, ye didn't really think we'd not go up after Matt right away? With ye bein' found alone we knew there must be something wrong. And ye so near dead, too. Well now, it wouldn't have done to have to bury ye without yer own uncle bein' here for the wake! We just had to go get him."

Rory bellowed with laughter. Matthew just looked at me and smiled.

He pulled something out from under my bunk. It was Dirk Black's pack.

"This Tom, you have to see to believe," he said. He turned it out beside me. As well as extra clothes, tobacco, powder, shot and whisky, there was a heavy moosehide bag full of coins, an oiled-silk parcel and a letter. I could barely use my peeling hands and I watched as Matthew opened the parcel. It held three neat stacks of

Bank of Montréal notes, all crisp and newly signed in amounts of five, ten and a hundred dollars. No less than $13,000. Over £3,000! The bag held silver dollars — Spanish and American — some half-dollars and pistareens, and half a dozen gold sovereigns — another $300 in hard cash.

"It's Colonel By's," I said, and I told Matthew of my last encounter with Dirk Black. He listened without a word. At the end he said: "You know, Tom, I thought all your talk of Dirk Black was something in your imagination. I didn't understand. I thought that shipwreck must have twisted your mind." He shook his head. "Well, the Colonel will get his money back."

The letter was next. It was addressed in a fine, even, ornate hand to "Master Thomas Penny, Chats Falls, in care of Wright's Post Office, Lower Canada."

"Seal was broken, Tom," Matthew said. "Black must have read it. Here — it's yours."

He held it for me. At the bottom of the page, underneath the clerk's careful writing, was the signature. It was thick and black and firmly scrawled — as clear and bold as the man himself. It was signed: "Jamie MacPherson."

Haltingly, I read it aloud:

Dear Tom Penny:

I have just received a letter from Alec Mac-Tavish. He sent it by the first downbound canoe he met, so it took a time to reach me

— just before freeze-up.

He had a good look over your land after he dropped you off at the Chats. He confirms it to be the right location for a canal cut to get by the Falls. Your neighbours, the Shirreffs, have come into partnership with me to develop the waterway and we would like to buy your land. I enclose my cheque on the Bank of Montréal for £3,000 made out to your uncle.

We really only need to use the waterfront including your swamp and pond so if you wish to keep the rest for your own purposes, we will simply reduce the sale price accordingly.

The cheque with Jamie's signature was pinned to the page. Three thousand pounds! The letter went on:

I am dispatching this by hand of Dirk Black, a seaman who had been injured and who worked very industriously in my warehouse these last two months.

Yes, I thought, Dirk Black could make a fine impression, even on one as observant as Jamie MacPherson!

You and I have a mutual friend — you call him Monsieur Untel, and I have known him for many years.

He told me how you stood by the men who helped you and that you would not take your share of money which you felt

*was illegally gained. It is an honour to me,
Tom Penny, to count a tough and honest
man like you among my friends.*

I looked at Matthew. His eyes were still hollow, but their sparkle had come back. We'd been through so much this last year. I could hardly grasp it all.

"Land for the summer — all we need for our farm," I murmured, "and money for lumbering, too — and more."

"Yes, Tom. This Jamie MacPherson knows what he wants and he's prepared to pay for it, and he's a generous man into the bargain. You've earned a good friend there."

I said: "Admiral Hardcastle helped him years ago, you know, when he was younger than I am. He hasn't forgotten it."

"And the Admiral's still the gentleman he always was, Tom. Look. There was a letter for me, too — from Will. He'll be finished in May — a qualified shipwright! The Admiral's getting him a passage out in a King's ship straight away. Just watch us Pennys then, eh? Farming, lumbering — and with Will here we could even build steamers for Jamie MacPherson and the Shirreffs!"

We lazed happily in the warmth of the first spring sunshine and waited for the river to break. Strength flowed back. My feet and my hands were useful again. Matthew swung about briskly on crutches, his leg on the mend.

Chipmunks ventured bright-eyed from their winter crannies and foraged about the camp. The ravens croaked, harsh-voiced. Redwings flashed and whistled by the frozen creek where the willows glowed yellow in the slanting sun. I could hear the water running down the slopes beneath the last of the snow.

Underneath my tender feet, through the thin skin of my moccasins, the soft ground had a different feel. It lived. It was mine. I knew it now, really knew it. This whole, wild land. It was where I lived, where I belonged.

At last the pent-up river burst the ice jam at the top of Paugan Falls. It started with a crack and a roar and a rumble that echoed, re-echoed and grew and grew.

"She's gone!" Shouts through the camp joined the river noise.

High up the falls the giant ice blocks lurched and tumbled. A mighty wall of ice and water hurtled down the rocky chute. Chunks the size of houses leaped and rolled and crashed upon the river ice below. In front of us the surface lifted as we watched. It heaved and cracked and broke. Great slabs reared up and churned and rolled. At once the river boiled with moving, grinding, crushing ice as far as we could see.

For hours, the ice-filled water rushed and roared, and frantic action filled the camp.

And then the ice was gone. The crew, like demons, hit the stacks of great squared timbers piled along the shore. Down they splashed — our winter's treasure — into the rushing Gatineau. The canoes then, with the drive crew, cant-hooks, pike-poles, paddles — all of us heading down, racing with the current, shouting, laughing, herding timber.

The drive was on, and we were going home.

Glossary

bark-mark: an identifying symbol lumbermen marked on their logs, originally using an axe.

binnacle: the housing containing the steering compass. It also holds a lamp to illuminate the compass card.

boule: ball.

bourgeois: a business or professional person. In the fur trade, the clerk in charge of a canoe brigade.

bowsprit: a spar projecting forward from the bow of a sailing ship.

brigade: a flotilla of fur trade canoes.

bulkhead: a partition.

bulwarks: a solid railing around a ship's side.

camboose: the sand hearth-fire and cooking area located in the centre of the "camboose shanty," the log building where the men lived. The word "shanty" alone referred to the whole camp. Timber rafts also had a camboose for cooking for the crew.

canaille: rabble, riffraff.

canot: canoe.

canot de maître **or Montréal canoe:** big thirty-six foot canoes used between Montréal and the lakehead.

canot du nord: canoe about twenty-five feet long generally used west of Lake Superior.

cant-hook: a pole with a movable hook near one

end used to grip and roll logs.

capote: a knee-length overcoat usually with a hood.

chat sauvage: raccoon (literally, wild cat).

dolphin-striker: an iron strut projecting downwards from the bowsprit.

doré: pickerel.

engagé: canoeman hired on contract.

fanny: a metal bucket for carrying food or drink.

fo'c's'le: short for forecastle, the forward part of the ship containing the crew's quarters.

gaff: spar extending back and upwards from the mast, supporting a fore-and-aft sail.

galley: ship's kitchen.

gars des hâches: axe-men.

halyard: rope for hoisting a sail.

Hard: a paved area sloping down into the water for loading boats and barges. In Portsmouth, the Hard is a sloping street on the harbour front.

hawse: an opening forward in a ship through which the anchor cable passes.

hovels: crude stables for oxen.

jamais: never.

lee side: the side away from the wind.

luff: the forward edge of a sail.

mangeurs de lard: pork eaters. The voyageurs who paddled the route from Montréal to the western end of Lake Superior lived on peas, corn and salt pork. Those who worked in the northwest beyond Lake Superior had a diet mainly of pemmican (dried pounded buffalo meat).

nouveau riche: one who has recently made his own money, rather than inheriting it.

Orangeman: an Irish Protestant; member of a secret society founded in Ireland in 1686 to uphold Protestantism. Named after William III, King of England, Prince of Orange.

parvenu: an upstart.

pays d'en haut: the northwest country.

peltries: skins, pelts.

pipe: each hour paddling was stopped for a few minutes for pipes to be lit. Distances were measured in "pipes," e.g., "*trois pipes*" was a three-hour paddle or about eighteen miles.

piqueteur: leading axe-man in charge of felling trees and marking them for squaring.

pistareen: a Spanish two-real coin (25 cents). The Spanish silver dollar, in world-wide common use in the seventeenth and eighteenth centuries, was worth eight reals (hence "pieces of eight"). The British pound sterling was the official currency in Canada, but any coins were accepted as legal tender.

poteen: Irish home-made whisky.

p't-être: (peut-être) perhaps.

scoop roof: a roof made with logs that were split, hollowed and placed side by side, one facing up, the next facing down and interlocking with each other like roof tiles to shed water.

scuppers: openings along the ship's side to drain

water from the deck.

scuttle: (not for coal!); a porthole or opening which can be closed when required.

shanty: lumber camp (from the French *chantier*).

sheet: rope attached to the lower corner of a sail to control its set.

ship in irons: a sailing vessel lying head to wind, unable to turn either way. The sails shudder in the wind.

spreader: strut projecting sideways from the mast to hold the stays outwards.

sternsheets: the after part of a small boat.

strop: a band of rope.

taffrail: rail around a vessel's stern.

thwart: a seat or a brace extending across a boat.

trammel: an iron hanger for holding pots over the fire.

tumpline: a line with a strap passing around the forehead for pulling a load or supporting a pack on the back.

watch: a four-hour period of duty. Morning watch — four a.m. to eight a.m. Dogwatch — a two-hour watch. The "first dog" is four a.m. to six p.m., the "last dog" six p.m. to eight p.m.